# Shelter
## for a
# Seabird

# Terry Farish

# Shelter
## for a
# Seabird

GREENWILLOW BOOKS
NEW YORK

Printed in the United States of America

First Edition   10 9 8 7 6 5 4 3 2 1

Library of Congress Cataloging-in-Publication Data
Farish, Terry.
Shelter for a seabird.
Summary: At a time when her stern father seems
determined to sell the island home where
her family has lived for generations, sixteen-
year-old Andrea is swept into a doomed romance
with a nineteen-year-old AWOL soldier.
[1. Islands—Fiction]   I. Title.
PZ7.F22713Sh    1990    [Fic]
89-25776    ISBN 0-688-09627-1

FOR STEVE
and
FOR CLIFFORD DICKERSON,
a harelegger who taught me
to love his island

# CONTENTS

CHAPTER 1 Ticket Office   1

CHAPTER 2 "Safe-in-Port"   10

CHAPTER 3 Company Supper   24

CHAPTER 4 Hot Cross Buns   32

CHAPTER 5 Popper   42

CHAPTER 6 Esther's Creperie   54

CHAPTER 7 Heron Beach   65

CHAPTER 8 The Mortician   73

CHAPTER 9 Least Tern   83

CHAPTER 10 Easter   90

CHAPTER 11 Tattoos   100

CHAPTER 12 The Fifties Dance   111

CHAPTER 13 Wake   120

CHAPTER 14 Payne House   126

CHAPTER 15 First Place   135

CHAPTER 16 Babies   144

CHAPTER 17 Low Tide   155

# Shelter
## for a
# Seabird

# CHAPTER 1

# Ticket
# Office

ANDREA HAD HAD A BABY and forsworn boys by the time she was sixteen and Swede came to the island. She had gone back to school, but she'd lost over three months having her baby girl. She felt like she'd been to war, and when Mr. Markworthy talked about transcendental poetry while he tapped his tennis shoes passionately, the words washed over her. She heard the foot and the clock. Sometimes she heard a baby.

At home she made tourist shirts. She made them from plain white shirts, which she washed to make the cotton soft. She painted on the soft cotton and sometimes studded them with jewels. She put jewel eyes on the fishes and bejeweled the tail feathers of birds.

Manhanset Island was no place for a girl to be fifteen, just out of her sophomore year, and pregnant. The island-born were mostly English with Calvinism in their genes. Andrea's family was practical, unsentimental, and ungiving. If she intended to have that baby, she would have it out of their sight. And she did. When the baby girl was born, Andrea gave her up for adoption. And when Andrea came back to the island from the maternity home, her parents didn't ask a single question.

Andrea had been home barely two months by Easter time. Her body still wasn't like other girls' bodies. She thought it never would be, now. Her belly and breasts were still round.

Andrea knew it was a family named Stuhr who was building next door to her on the creek. None of her family had met them except her Uncle Clint, whom they hired to do the building. When Swede Stuhr called, that was the first they knew of a son. Swede told them he had some leave—he was in the Army—and he wanted to come see the house. He called to beg a ride from the ferry.

Andrea's parents, Sterling and Bess, couldn't figure it. They brooded over the visit as if the boy was being sent to spy or in some way butt in on Clint's work. It was still early in the spring and work had been slow with all the rain.

When Andrea first saw Swede, he was leaning over an arcade game in the Cross Sound Ferry ticket office. He was staring at the game lights and was so still, she thought they might have borrowed a part of his brain. He wore owl-eye specs with reflector lenses and BDUs, bloused at the boots.

Andrea put sixty-five cents in the vending machine and got a milky coffee. Swede was an errand, one more thing to pick up for her mother.

"Andrea Tagg?" he asked, peering over his owl eyes at her.

"Swede?" she answered.

He bowed. Then he went back to shoving the joysticks on the arcade machine.

The Stuhrs were from the Midwest but liked the ocean and came exploring the East Coast in their yacht. They moored in the harbor of Manhanset Island, the island-town sheltered between the north and south forks of Long Island and named for its first people, the tribe of Manhansets. The Stuhrs bought land one year by Andrea's house and began plans to build. People who sailed large yachts did that sort of thing, Andrea knew, after they discovered her island.

But Swede couldn't live in a house with no walls or ceilings, only beams and the outline of rooms you had to catwalk across. Andrea had watched the frame of the house go up over the two months she'd been back. She catwalked across all its room frames and doorways; she planned the kitchen, the bedrooms, and a room she claimed for animals and tired birds. Uncle Clint was the builder. She knew the guy who was going to build the cupboards after they got the wallboard up. Andrea had

3

watched and thought if a person happened to be a carpenter, they might do all right on the island. Otherwise they were in trouble.

Andrea liked the smell of new lumber there on the creek where they lived, and she had come to like what Uncle Clint was making next door. Their own place was rotting. It wasn't that she was mellowing on summer people. She hated them as hotly as her father did. But there was something so good and healthy about the smell of that new-cut pine.

Swede didn't know there wasn't any roof on the house until that morning when he called Bess to say he could use a ride because his car had broken down. Bess ended up inviting him to stay with them. Andrea knew it wasn't out of the goodness of her heart. It was more like duty. She and Sterling would have found it too uncomfortable not to at least ask him. "Do not curse the rich," Sterling had muttered, "even in your bedroom."

Andrea glanced at Swede in the ticket office. He had muscular, hairy arms. He had more hair on his arms than he had on his head. He was fair-haired and all he had was fuzz. She could see his scalp. He had stripes, four zigzags above his ear. She almost wanted fuzz so she could shave designs on her head too. Her hair was now moonlight blond. Last summer she had been a pastel blond. She and her best friend, Polly, took Polaroids of each other for color checks. By New Year's she was reddish brown because they wouldn't let her put any colors on her hair at the maternity home.

4

She sat back and let her eyes shift to a man with CAP-
TAIN BOB'S CHARTER FISHING printed on his jacket. He
and some other fishermen played country-western songs
on the jukebox.

Swede ambled to her bench. She looked at his BDUs
and his fuzz. Everybody did. He was a performance.
"Good fishing?" he called to the man in the Captain Bob
jacket.

"Not bad lobstering," Captain Bob said. "Now that the
ice is broke." Captain Bob looked them over and gave
Swede his card.

The soldier and Andrea were odd enough. Swede managed to look like a skinhead in a soldier's costume, and
Andrea was tall, big-boned, with a lot of moonlight blond
hair and paint all over her like war paint. She was an artist
and smelled like turpentine.

She watched Captain Bob, and then she watched the
woman selling ferry tickets. She had a braid down her back
like a girl, but her face was not a girl's face.

There was no music in Andrea's house. She didn't mind
sitting in the ticket office, watching the people and listening to the jukebox.

"How's the house coming?" Swede asked her.

"It's coming," she said.

"I've been in a Sheridan tank," he said. "It's got to beat
a tank."

Andrea slurped the coffee and tapped her palm against
her jeans to the music. The woman with the braid walked

over to shut a window, and the fishermen's eyes followed her.

Swede looked toward the door. "They let me go just in time to make the boat. Why don't we go and I can get out of these clothes."

She shrugged and looked down the pier at a sandpiper and a rusted trawler with the name *Illusions* on its hull. She liked the music. "After I finish," she told him, and slumped into the bench.

She listened to Captain Bob and some truckers talk.

"You want to get going?" Swede said.

"Relax," she said.

He said, "I can't understand a word they're saying."

"What do you mean?"

"The way you people talk. Like you're mad as hell. You kind of spit words at each other."

"You'll get used to it," she told him.

Swede had one bag. He tossed it on Andrea's bench. He looked at his watch. He rubbed his fuzz with the heel of his hand. Then he sat down, took off his glasses, and looked at her. She was aware that he was studying her turquoise triangle earrings. They were wooden and they clacked. He looked at her T-shirt. She was wearing her purple goat shirt. On it was a picture of a goat that looked like he was about to burp. Underneath it read: "Mow Your Own Grass." She wore it for weekenders and summer people whose needs were endless, like the Stuhrs.

Swede said, "Nothing personal, but I'm on business."

She looked at him. She knew she could effect an icy gray

stare. Her father could, and she'd grown up hearing her eyes were a match for her father's. She gave Swede her iciest look.

He sat back. He talked about his house. He said, "I've got to do a lot of measurements and calculations." She half expected him to whip out a pocket calculator. But then he seemed to give up on her and he slung the strap of his bag over his shoulder, more like a student than a soldier, and went out the door. Andrea drank her coffee. She figured he couldn't get far. When she was ready, she followed him down the pier past *Illusions*. The old planks smelled thickly of creosote and squealed under their feet.

They drove in from the tip of Long Island to Baytown, where they pulled onto the North Ferry. Since bridges had been built, there had been talk of building one from the mainland to Manhanset Island. But in the end nobody really wanted a bridge. It was fifteen minutes by ferry to the mainland. Islanders thought that was fast enough. They had doctors, a supermarket, and a small business district by the harbor. Some people never left the island and would be satisfied if a ferry came, say, Tuesdays. Just a small thread to the rest of the world.

Sul was on duty. He was an old bass fisherman who'd lucked out and gotten a ferry job when the government brought an end to men seining for bass. He touched his eyebrow in salute when he saw Andrea and packed their car in tight. Swede seemed to get bored halfway across and closed his eyes. Andrea thought coming in on a ferry must have been dull compared to sailing in, real tight to the wind. She'd watched people do that and then let their sails luff under Payne House and the Harbor Pastry Shop, where they sold flaky French things and hand-painted earrings to the tourists.

After she drove down the ramp and onto the island, Swede all but hung out the window into the cold as though he had been starving for air.

"Why don't you put on the radio?" he said.

"There isn't any radio."

So Swede sang. He howled a Queen song out the window as they passed the rolling lawn of Payne House, the old, white-shingled hotel with a wraparound porch and a nouveau French cuisine.

Swede said, "Wait a minute, stop the car. Here's music."

Andrea stopped the car and Swede ran up the wrought-iron steps to the main entrance, thundering in his battle boots and chanting the entire Payne House menu in pretty good French.

Andrea listened. She was having a hard time catching up in her French class. She was failing most of her classes, except her drawing class. She was maybe borderline in geometry. She was running out of time and she knew it. She sat expressionless in the car waiting for another off-the-wall summer kid to finish expressing himself. She hoped her mother was getting paid a bed-and-breakfast fee, and a chauffeur's fee, too.

"God, I'm hungry," Swede said when he came back.

8

She couldn't imagine what he was doing in the Army. She didn't care, either.

He said, "You wonder why I joined up. My dad sees it as a sort of French Foreign Legion. Last chance to shape me up. Or get wasted."

"Shut the door," she said. "I'm on business, too."

# CHAPTER 2

# "Safe-in-Port"

THEY ARRIVED AT HER OWN old brown house on the creek. It was sea-weathered cedar and had ragged yellow awnings over the windows.

Andrea and her sister, Eleanore, had always lived there. Sterling had always lived there. Popper, her grandfather, had been born there, and her grandmother had died in the front room while her children played cards at the kitchen table. The Tagg house used to be the only house on the creek. All the land used to be cauliflower and potato fields. But now Bess and Andrea grew sweet corn and strawberries because that's what sold to people in the lodges and the summer homes. Cookout food. There wasn't a head of cauliflower to be seen.

It was a dowdy, unstylish house, the kind nobody looked at twice. A small wooden sign hung beside the front door, where lilacs would spread and hide the words from May until September. The sign read "SAFE-IN-PORT." The Taggs never tackled the high seas. They were farmers. The most they ever had was a two-person skiff. Popper had something he called a catboat, which he and their neighbor, Wush Huckins, took out when they fished with a hand seine. But the words "SAFE-IN-PORT" must have pleased Popper's heart, Andrea always thought. Something from all those years of Christian Endeavor the island kids went to at church during the Depression. So the house wore the name "SAFE-IN-PORT," even though that would fit a mighty ship or a headstone.

Swede wasn't looking at the Taggs' house. He had found the frame of his own roof, which soared above the willows.

Sterling came out the front door, hiking up his pants. He wore cowboy boots and walked across the brown grass as if he were killing moles. He had angry eyes. When he looked at her, Andrea thought, no matter if she was only watching the sunset, he still looked mad, as though she couldn't even do that right. He stuck out his hand to Swede.

Swede took it in his strong hand and smiled so beguilingly, Andrea thought he might ask her father for a date.

Sterling looked up at his fuzz for a long while before he mumbled hello. He nodded toward Swede's house. "Couldn't you make it no bigger?" he said. "You made it a little bigger, you coulda blocked out the stars and the moon, too." Sterling's eyes were gray and the skin around them crinkled, but they were not smile lines.

"Yeah, it's big," Swede said good-naturedly. "It's my mother's dream house."

Sterling lit a cigarette and sheltered it in the cup of his hand. He liked to talk, Andrea knew; here was an audience. "My brother's been working hard. Got it framed, and now he's starting to rough it in and do the fine work. You ought to see how some of these places go up."

Andrea shifted her weight and looked now and then in Sterling's stony eyes while he talked, and then he got in his pickup and his tires spit out gravel as he drove away.

"I'm going to go have a look," Swede said, and headed for the road.

Andrea would have gone back to her own house, but she was unable to get her father's angry eyes and the sound as he ripped through the gravel out of her mind. Instead of going in, she took a shortcut through a stand of pines and past the Taggs' chicken house. It led down a well-used path edged with greenbrier and bayberry. At the end of the path was the pine skeleton of the Stuhrs' enormous home. She felt oddly close to all those boards. In the daytime they belonged to Clint and his crew, but at dawn and at night they were hers.

She stopped by the path and noticed the kid with her Uncle Clint. She picked a bayberry and crushed it and lifted her fingers to her nose to smell the fragrance. Swede walked around the whole place. He kicked at rocks. He threw clamshells across the creek. He stepped inside and gazed upward at what would be the cathedral ceiling. "Looks good to me," she heard him call.

Uncle Clint came down the ladder and Andrea watched them talk. They pointed and raised and lowered their voices. Clint spit. Swede scuffed.

Swede was not tall but he was broad shouldered, and when he walked inside the house, looking at joints and ballasts and door frames, he seemed big. And Swede in his bloused BDUs made it seem like an invasion.

"Just look at it," he called to her because he had seen her there.

"I've been looking at it," she said. "I saw it when it was a pit. Then they brought in the lumber, load after load." She remembered how good that new-sawed wood smelled when she got home. "And then the birds came. It's real popular with the sea hawks. I'd build them a deck there," she said, pointing to the rafters.

"My mother's gone to the trouble of drawing up plans."

Andrea shrugged. "It's where I'd put the deck," she said.

"Don't tell her," he said. "She gets nasty when anybody has thoughts on her plans."

"Is she coming, too?"

"God help me if she does," Swede said. He came out on what would be a second-story balcony. "It's going to be hard to measure the windows." He whipped an imaginary tape measure out of his back pocket to measure the space where a window would be.

"It'd be hard to put up curtains, too. Tell your mother."

13

"If my mother wants to put up curtains, not having windows won't stop her."

Andrea turned back down the path, smelling the heavy scent of bayberry as she walked. She liked the house empty.

Andrea stood in front of the mirror in her own living room. It was framed in dark wood with tile inlays. It had been her grandmother's mirror, too, the one who died in the double cherry bed they brought downstairs so she could look out the window with a good view of the creek. Andrea looked at herself in the mirror. She could wear her old jeans, but they cut into her belly. Her shirts weren't so baggy. She looked in the mirror and thought of her grandmother and the little baby she'd given away. She felt permanently different in body and mind.

She tried to be the same friend she was to Polly as she had been before she went away. But she was marked. It wasn't bad to have had a baby; it was just a little disgusting when it should have been easy enough to fix it. All that blood and pain.

She never missed the boy. He was only a summer kid. It was only one time. Andrea's parents thought it was better not even to tell the boy. She thought they would have been embarrassed to have to meet his parents. So the boy didn't even know he was a father. She thought at least she knew she was a mother.

It was never the boy she missed; it was her friend Polly. She missed Polly more than the world. Polly was still

14

there, but it was different. Polly didn't have a belly that had grown a baby girl, and Polly hadn't been in labor for eighteen hours, chanting, "Oh, shit, oh, shit, oh, shit."

Andrea went in the kitchen, which she had made into a shirt shop with her tubes of paints and pots for mixing them. Polly said she might come over, but Andrea didn't think she would. She and Polly used to experiment with T-shirt designs and had found an incredibly easy and popular one using two bare footprints, preferably Polly's, because even her feet were petite.

Polly used to bring beauty aids when they were twelve because her mother worked in a beauty shop. Once Polly brought a crimper and makeup. She sat on the porch look-ing in a compact mirror and turned herself from a skinny kid in a sweatshirt into a movie star. Then she and Andrea smeared violet eye shadow and blush all over themselves. They combed their eyebrows up to accentuate the arch. Then they lay on their bellies on the dock and talked about sex.

Andrea remembered Polly telling her that her lips were too fat, and she said, So are yours, and Polly drew a line of purple lipstick inside her real lips. She held up a mirror like they do at the beauty shop.

Sometimes Polly had stayed over, and they slept in Grandma Tagg's cherry bed. They took turns lying on top of each other—giggly girls—bottom to bottom, giggling and howling. "Is that how they do it?" Polly would howl. "How should I know?" Andrea would howl back. "It can't be how they do it."

15

Andrea was nostalgic for the time when she and Polly had been innocent together. But Polly wasn't coming, so Andrea put her own feet in the basin of yellow paint, which was where they were when Swede came in the kitchen door.

He said, "I get faint when I don't eat."

She glanced up at his husky body. "There's the fridge," she said.

Swede began taking out small plastic containers. He shoved her paints off half the kitchen table and began filling it with cold spaghetti and wedges of meat loaf and a bowl of baked custard as big as Block Island. He sat down to eat.

"Don't they have food in Sheridan tanks?"

Swede shook his head. His mouth was crammed with spaghetti and meatballs. He smeared cold sauce off his chin and shoved in some more. He ate all the meat loaf.

"What are you doing?" he said. He watched her step from the paint to a shirt.

"Nothing," she said. "It's a shirt."

"Why'd you step on it?"

"Your room's upstairs," she said. "The first room you see straight ahead."

Andrea stepped off the shirt and left two perfect, golden, arched footsteps. She rinsed off her feet one at a time in the kitchen sink.

Swede said, "You should stop jumping around. You're making plaster drop in my spaghetti."

Andrea glanced at the ceiling and saw, sure enough, more bits of plaster falling.

16

He ate half of the Block Island of custard.

Andrea knew the kitchen linoleum curled from the corners. She knew in the living room you could see all the layers of the house, down to the lath boards. You could see Great-grandma's rose wallpaper under Popper's stripes, and over that a coating of soldier-blue paint.

She hung the shirt to dry on a hanger, and a bit of waxed paper that had separated the layers of cotton fluttered to the floor. She spread another one on the table, well away from his spaghetti sauce. On it were two cartoon kids with curly hair lying on their bellies in the surf.

Andrea stirred up more colors in the compartments of a cupcake tin.

"I guess there's more people in your family?" he asked.

"I guess," Andrea said. She put rosy cheeks on the cartoon children and polish on the girl's toenails. She wished the boy would go away. She worked with her eyes hidden behind her hair like a child.

Soon he stopped trying to get her to talk and took his bag upstairs.

"Which room?" he yelled.

"First room. Straight ahead."

She heard his bag drop to the floor. He came down the stairs. She knew he had found the barest amount of furniture. Bess had been spring-cleaning. She took a lot of stuff up to the church bring-and-buy. She said sooner or later somebody would buy their place up, and Andrea had kidded her about somebody turning their house into a tearoom or somebody would sell slushes out the kitchen

17

window. Andrea did not believe her father was looking to sell out. They were one with that house.

Swede went in the living room and Andrea heard him open the porch door. She knew all the doors of the house by their groans and squeaks. She was lucky to have grown up on the creek, the kids at school who lived in the center always told her. She didn't think of it as lucky. It was just who she was. She was a Tagg on Tagg Creek. Now she was a Tagg on Tagg Creek who had been to war and come home to the familiar squeaking porch door. It was her brown grass that dropped to her crooked, muddy creek, even though her creek was much narrower when she came home than before she left. Sterling said that was nonsense. Always been no more than fifty feet, not counting the spring tides, when sometimes it pulled in skinny as a furrow.

Andrea could hear the top porch step squeal when Swede sat down on it. He was singing and drumming the wood. She'd been hanging the next shirt on the door to the staircase when she saw him. He drummed and smoothed back his fuzz, as if he were still used to having hair on the side of his head.

He glanced around when she was looking and grinned at her. He had taken off his combat boots and was barefoot. "I shouldn't be here," he said. "I should be in my tank."

She wanted to say, "So go the hell back." But she just turned around.

"My mother always wanted me to come and see their cottage."

Andrea stopped. "She calls it a cottage?"

"Yeah, that thing's a cottage."

Andrea could hear Uncle Clint's hammer. The Stuhrs brought gold for Uncle Clint's pockets. That's what the summer people did.

"If I had any sense, I wouldn't hang around here," Swede said. But he didn't move. He sat rubbing his head with his palm. Andrea thought he'd worry away what hair he had.

"I've got to get out of these clothes!" He was barreling down the brown grass to the creek in his white bare feet. "This is what I think of the goddamn Army!" he hollered. He tore the green T-shirt off and threw it in the creek. He wrenched his belt out of its loops and threw his belt in the creek. He hurled his boots in the creek. And he unzipped his jungle pants and threw them in the creek. The hammering from the roof of the Stuhr cottage cut off the way music blasting from a radio gets cut off. That's when Andrea looked at Swede's face. His face was stiff. He didn't see Andrea when he trudged up from the creek, his heels pounding in the grass, in nothing but his shorts and a body covered with goose bumps from the island air, which wasn't much warmer than freezing.

She could not imagine why a rich summer kid should look like rage. She could tell him about rage. He bored her and she turned and went back to the kitchen.

She wondered where Eleanore was and remembered she must be with their mother. She thought about calling Polly because it was so dead lonely during the Easter holidays. She called six times before the line wasn't busy.

19

"Who's the soldier?" Polly asked right off.

"Nobody. He just needed a ride."

"To your house?"

"Look, Polly, I didn't call about him."

"Is he staying with you?"

"He has Eleanore's room for a couple nights. What's going on, Polly?"

"Nothing much. Jen and I are sort of studying. But mostly we're deciding who . . ." Peals of Jen's and Polly's laughter bounced joyously over the phone lines. ". . . who . . ." More laughter. ". . . who we're going to fall in love with. We decided we're tired of not being in love. Everybody we know is in love."

"I'm not," said Andrea.

"No," Polly said. She stopped laughing.

Jen got on. "I picked the guy I saw you on the ferry with."

"You can have him."

"What's his name?"

"Swede. Come and get him."

"What is he, Swedish?"

"How should I know?"

"You didn't ask him?"

The conversation didn't get any better. Jen and Polly kept collapsing in laughter that all but shook the telephone until Andrea said she had to go.

By suppertime Andrea had five T-shirts drying on the counters, hanging over drawers, tossed onto the torn linoleum floor. Sterling worked at the boat yard across the creek. She hoped her mother and Eleanore beat him home. In case they didn't, she decided to be out of the way. She hated when it was just the two of them. He would take his paper to whatever room she wasn't in. He seemed embarrassed to know her, as if she were nursing a baby in his presence or some other disgusting thing to do with her body.

She put on Sterling's jacket. It was scratchy wool on the outside and thick flannel on the inside, and she took it off the hook on the back of the door whenever Sterling didn't wear it. She got Bess's egg basket and went out to collect eggs. It was dusk.

She walked through the briers where the salt roses would bloom and where the pitch pines grew, slanted from the pressure of the sea breeze. She heard a screech and looked up to see a bird with an enormous wingspan gliding with the sky as a backdrop. It was a sea hawk.

It was probably the sea hawk, she thought, who built a nest up where the new roof peaked. She looked up toward the roof and thought she heard a hammering, not like when Clint worked. It was a less sure sound. But it was coming from the roof. She walked down the bayberry path. When she got to the house, it was the boy, Swede, she saw on the roof. He was hammering down the plywood where Clint had left off.

"What are you doing?" she said. "You don't know how to do that."

"Yeah, I do. Your uncle showed me. Jeez, this feels good to be up here." He looked toward the sky and pounded his chest. Then he went back to hammering.

"I know he didn't tell you to do it in the dark."

Swede kept on hammering.

"A sea hawk family just built a nest up there."

"Is that what that ugly bird was? I'll remember this place for having the number-one ugly bird."

"The sea hawks just came back," she said. "They come March twenty-first every year. And if that nest isn't there tomorrow—" She stopped. What could she threaten him with?

He said, "I won't hammer any ugly birds."

Andrea walked down to the creek. It was low tide and she scuffed the toes of her shoes across the wet sand, leaving a trail like a turtle's. She didn't think she'd ever felt so hopeless. She hurt. Her heart hurt, or something in her. Something physically hurt.

It was dark in the henhouse, and she felt through the straw and squawking hens for their eggs.

"How does a bird know when it's March twenty-first?"

She looked up at the boy. She wanted very much to hate him. She wanted to hate him the way she hated Markworthy and her father and the nurses at the maternity home. But she felt so tired and hopeless. It was almost easier not to hate him.

"It's true, though," she said. The boy had on what soldiers called their civvies since he'd thrown all his jungle clothes in the creek. He had on baggy pants and a striped shirt. "They know when it's March, and they come and all the bird crazies get out their guns to shoot anybody who looks cross-eyed at a sea-hawk nest or a tern nest on the beaches."

22

He said, "But it's so ugly."

"I'll show you ugly," she said. "Come see my rooster."

She swung open the top half of a Dutch door, scattering straw over them both.

"Got his own room?" Swede said.

"Mom doesn't want the hens going broody."

"God, no," Swede said.

"Hey, Jimmy," she called, as if Jimmy were a dog. "Hey, Jimmy-Jimmy-Jimmy-bird. Maybe he got out," she said to Swede. "Sometimes I find him up to your place."

But Jimmy didn't come flapping his wings to sit on the door ledge. Swede felt through the cold straw for eggs, too. Andrea wrapped her fingers around them to warm herself before she placed them in the basket.

She kept looking through the door to the other side and calling for the rooster. "Dad gave him to me when we found out he wasn't a hen. You'll hear him for sure about five in the morning."

# CHAPTER 3

# COMPANY SUPPER

WHEN THEY STEPPED OUT OF the henhouse, there was only sound, willow branches rubbing against one another in the cold wind and water lapping against the barrels Sterling used to lay a dock. Bess called, "Andy! Andy . . ." It was the same way she called when Andrea was a little kid.

She and the boy walked through the black pitch pines. The triangles of Andrea's wooden earrings clacked.

They stepped into a blast of warm cooking smells in the Tagg kitchen. Bess Tagg was whipping milk into a skillet of drippings. She stopped long enough to give Swede a look-over and mutter something about his being welcome.

Eleanore sat on the kitchen counter in a man-size apron,

swinging her legs and staring at Swede. She kept on staring until he spoke to her.

"You smell like grape," he said.

She held up her decorated arms. "Grape Magic Marker," she said. She had drawn hearts and diamonds up and down her arms.

"Enough," Bess said. "Wash that mess off your hands and call Dad for supper."

"Not me," Eleanore said. "Dad won't stop talking on the phone to listen to me. He's talking about the moon. He said somebody offered him the moon for our house."

Andrea looked up from laying the silverware to glance at her mother's face. It was one thing for Eleanore to joke. What did she know about real estate? But her mother wouldn't look at her. She didn't tell Eleanore, "Enough of that nonsense."

"Mom?" Andrea said.

Her mother's face was soft. Andrea had touched it when she came back from the shelter home. She had wanted to hug her but Bess was very busy, so she had only touched her face. Bess had long arched eyebrows. She didn't wear makeup and her only vanity was keeping her eyebrows perfectly plucked. She had a girlish habit of wearing her hair pushed off her face with a hair band. Now when Andrea looked at her, she saw soft pursed lips, and for the first time Andrea thought of the possibility of her family's selling this frumpy, brown, middle-aged-lady house.

"Sterling," Bess called. She hadn't answered Andrea.

"Sterling, come on while it's hot." She also forgot about Eleanore's armadillo arms.

Sterling swaggered in. He sat down and began telling Swede about island history. Bess dropped a plate of store-bought bread on the table. Swede took a slice. "Excuse me. Would you like some bread?" he said to Sterling.

Sterling helped himself and said, "It all began after the war. Every week a new developer'd come along. Nobody came along for nothing before the war. Farmers had a hard time selling their crops at the point."

Andrea thought he made it seem that the Taggs had not seen an outsider for several centuries. She sat down.

"Nothing worked," Sterling said. "The Agricultural Co-op lasted about a year. My grandfather lost every cent he put in it. It never had a chance."

"Never did," said Bess.

She put a plate of boiled chicken and steamed dumplings on the table.

"Cheap bastards on this island," Sterling was saying. He served the chicken. He served around the white and dark meat as if it were all the same. There wasn't much of it for five people.

"Eleven eggs is all there was in the basket," Bess said.

"It was dark, Mom."

"I was hoping for three dozen to take up tomorrow."

"The dessert chef only uses Mom's eggs," Eleanore told Swede. "He says her eggs work magic."

"Where?" Swede said. "Not that place we passed with five stars on their menu?"

That pleased Bess. Her eyes almost smiled.

"They'll tell you if you go," Sterling said. "They only use farm-fresh eggs from island farms, and that's Bess's."

"I want to go," Eleanore said.

"Sure," Sterling said. "You can go as a window washer if you're lucky."

"No eggs for the noodle heads at Payne," Eleanore sang.

"Eleanore Tagg," snapped Bess, and she got up for more bread, like she was feeding a flock of birds. All the chicken was gone.

"Where's Jimmy?" Andrea asked. "He wasn't in the back room."

Bess passed the peas. "He had no business in the back room to begin with," she said.

"You said you didn't want the hens to go broody."

"And he had no business in the front room."

"All right, so I'll keep him in a box in my room."

"Andrea, you are sixteen years old, not a little naive child. Jimmy wasn't doing us any good. Company was coming for supper, and who can afford any standing rib roast or what have you on this island."

Bess retucked her salt-and-pepper hair underneath her hair band. "Jimmy wasn't doing anybody any good. You know we never meant to keep a rooster. He was only getting older and tougher. Tough enough as it was. Now, Andrea, clear the plates. Eleanore, you help her and I'll fix some coffee."

Andrea didn't move.

27

Andrea looked down at the strip of well-cooked meat that fell off the chicken bone on her pink china plate.

"Make that coffee strong," Sterling said. Andrea pressed her fists against her ears and made a wad of blond hair at the nape of her neck.

Bess walked to the sink and filled the kettle.

"This goddamn property is costing us more in taxes than I can squirrel together." Sterling kept talking while he chewed. "They treat you like dirt if you depend on this place for a living. You can only afford to live here if you weren't born here. You're done before you get started."

He shook salt from the shaker into his hand, sprinkled some on Jimmy, and tossed the rest over his shoulder. "For luck," Sterling said. He made a laughing sound, but his eyes stayed an icy gray. "Don't you try that," he said. He shook his gruff head at Eleanore, who was staring at her plate.

Andrea got up and threw her plate in the sink and ran upstairs. She went in the bathroom. She knew how chickens were killed. She knew how their necks were wrung. She pressed her fingers hard against the porcelain, waiting for that picture to get out of her mind. And the taste out of her mouth. "Oh, God," she whispered. She tried to flush the taste out with water she scooped with her hands.

She heard footsteps in the hall. It would be her father. She almost slammed the door, but she was too late. He was too close. It was Swede who came in, though, and she turned her back. He sat on the edge of the tub. She

28

thought she was going to throw up in front of a stranger, but she felt too sick to yell at him to get out. Andrea gripped the sink. Her fingers were as white as the porcelain. She felt the boy's hand warm on her back for one second.

"Worried about a dumb cock!" Sterling yelled from the kitchen. "How'd she get to be such a princess?"

The hand touched her back again.

"You think you can just get up and storm around this place." He was coming up the stairs. "You live with me by my good graces, understand? Or you pay me rent, understand? Just how much are you bringing in, how much does that girl, Esther, pay you? Not a hell of a lot. So you pay attention to your place here. Now go apologize to your mother for smashing that dish." He was at the bathroom door. Andrea would listen but she wouldn't make herself look in his eyes. "She was putting on a nice meal," Sterling said, "and you ruined it. I don't know what's gonna become of you. Squeaking by in everything you do and making a federal case out of a rooster."

"Sterling?" It was Bess on the stairs.

"You're another thing that's done before it got started," he said hoarsely.

The boy left sometime during the yelling. Bess came and shut the bathroom door and Andrea threw up in the toilet.

When the night was all dark, Andrea went to sit on the porch. She folded herself into a ball and rocked on the glider swing, wrapped in an afghan.

Swede came out. She didn't want to talk to him. She didn't want to listen to him, either. Why couldn't people realize when they were in the way?

He stood watching the creek with his hands shoved in his pockets. She almost forgot he was there until he said, "I shouldn't be here. God," he said, "I'm sorry."

"Well, God, I am sorry, too." She had no charity. "I wish you'd get the hell out of here. What did you come for? What are you going to do? String a hammock over at your mansion and crack your whip over my Uncle Clint? Maybe you'll wear a Panama hat and eat bing cherries or something. And get the locals to fan you."

She got up to leave. She wrapped the afghan tight around her hips. The bell buoys rang from the channel. Before she could open the door, Bess opened it. She stood in the doorway. She was framed by the living-room light behind her. She wore a gingham skirt that stood out around her shins. "A petticoat keeps it out," she told them, patting the ruffle at the hem. "Sterling's taking me to the fifties dance on Monday night. Thought I'd try this on."

Bess glanced toward the shadow that was Swede. "You must be asleep on your feet," she said.

"I'm fine," he said.

Andrea said, "I'm going to bed."

"You should," Bess said. "I'm going. I just wanted to show you my dress." She shut the door but only partway.

Andrea watched the lights roll on the water. She left Swede on the porch. She, and probably Bess, too, hoped he didn't want to spend his leave there after all. Maybe he would tack a nice note on the porch door and be gone by the time they had to get up again in the morning. Tomorrow was Good Friday. The island was bleak and brown, and she thought it was the unlikeliest name for a tomorrow she'd ever heard.

# CHAPTER 4

# HOT CROSS BUNS

IT WAS DAWN ON TAGG Creek, or what the Taggs called only the crick.

Andrea lay in her bed and listened to the gulls and an amplified mouse squeak that was one cry of the tern. She woke up thinking about Wush Huckins. Even if her heart wasn't in it, she could get her feet to walk down the blacktop to Wush's cottage, where she used to always go. When his wife, Winnie, was alive, she used to give Andrea homemade doughnuts. They were always at least two days old and crunchy on the outside and not all that soft on the inside, and Andrea still liked doughnuts best a little old. There was more to chew.

She leaned against the windowsill. The tide was in, the creek spread to its full, muddy path. She knew why she woke up. Jimmy wasn't shaking the creek with his crowing. She wanted to tell Wush. Wush had stories about hens and mules and working the land during the Depression. Wringing a rooster's neck was what they did on Sundays if they were lucky. Andrea knew that. But she hated the stillness of the morning.

She got up and pulled on one of her white T-shirts. It was soft. She'd bought a kimono made of that soft cotton, baby-sized, when she lived in the home. She'd bought it at Woolworth's. She wasn't sure why. It had been wrapped in plastic with cardboard between the front and back. When the baby was almost due, she wanted to buy her something. She looked at a bassinet and a music box even though she knew she would never see the baby. She bought the yellow kimono for the pure joy of paying the lady for it at the checkout.

She put on Sterling's scratchy jacket over her shirt and left by the front door. At least a real estate agent hadn't snuck over in the night and driven a for-sale sign with bouncy balloons into their front lawn. She'd seen plenty of those on the island this spring. She ran past the henhouse and down the bayberry path because she always went that way to see how the new house grew.

But she never looked at the house, because she saw something else. It was strung between two scrub pines like a huge green cocoon, hanging low to the ground. It

33

blocked her path, and she yelped when she almost fell into it. When she stepped back, she saw it raise its head.

It jerked up and screamed, "You moron! You just sailed over a mine. You just fried the whole fuckin' squad." Then it lay down.

"Swede?" she said.

He didn't answer. It was him. He was in a nylon olive-drab sleeping bag, and the sleeping bag was on some kind of tarp with ropes he'd tied to the trees. She could see his peach fuzz at the top with one of his hands slung out over his scalp. She could have told him to wake up if he wanted to get out of that tank, but she didn't want him there. She didn't want to hear his dreams.

"Why are you doing that?" she said. "What the hell are you doing?"

The hand pulled a flap of nylon off his face, and he squinted at her. He rubbed his eyes and looked at the luminous numbers on his watch.

"What you said," he finally said. "Only I don't have a Panama hat."

"Why?" she said. "Why don't you just go away? We haven't even been nice to you. Why are you being so nice back? Look at you. We don't need anybody around trying to charm the shit out of us."

Swede put his head back inside the sleeping bag.

She sat down on the stump where she always sat. It was her stump.

"Believe me, it's nothing personal. I need help," he said. "I think I'm AWOL."

Andrea burst out laughing.

"Great," he said. "I can really pick the sympathetic ones."

"It was the way you said it, like 'I think I'm pregnant.'"

"I just got on a bus at the Howard Johnson's," he said.

"I don't want to hear it." She got up.

He said, "I wanted to tell you since I saw you sitting there drinking your coffee at the ferry. I guessed it wouldn't seem so much like I might as well be dead if I told somebody. Before, I was thinking I might as well be dead."

She looked at where the nylon made a bump over his nose.

She said, "Of all the problems I've tried to think up answers to, I never tried to think up an answer to that one."

Swede pulled himself out of the sleeping bag. He buttoned a shirt over his undershirt and put on a jacket. He tied on a pair of running shoes. His feet were as long as flippers.

"Are there Army police after you?" Andrea asked.

"They don't do that anymore," he said. "But your squad starts to look."

She wrapped her arms around herself and shivered.

"It's not like we're at war," he said.

"It feels like war when you say that."

Swede stood with his thumbs propped low on his hips, watching the creek. "Place is a goddamn bird sanctuary," he said.

"Unless you're a rooster," she said, and started toward

35

the water. "You should see Heron Beach if you think there's a lot here."

"Okay, let's go."

"No, I was just going up to see somebody." She started back down to the beach but she glanced back. She saw him cram his sleeping bag under the tarp. Furrows cut across his forehead.

It was a cold, bright Good Friday. Andrea walked along the edge of the creek instead of walking down the blacktop road. She scuffed through shells and dry seaweed and smelled the heavy salty air and heard Swede's footsteps and knew he was following. Up past a new cedar chalet was Wush's small cottage, nearly on the creek's edge. It had no dock, no driveway, and no deck. It had two small rooms and a screened porch.

Andrea watched the terns. Now they sang a funny *kip-kip-kip* song. They had orange beaks, and when they flew, their wings opened out a splashy black cloak. She could see the boat yard where her father worked through a haze on the water. At Wush's a single crocus eased between a clam rake and a patch of grass.

By the time she knocked on Wush's door, Swede had come ambling, casually, hands in his pockets, owl specs back over his eyes, up from the creek. Inside, she could hear pots clink.

Wush's door was red and decked with a spring straw hat the way Winnie would have decked it. A polka-dot bow dangled from the hat's crown. Andrea knocked again. Wush's white head appeared, and one end of the bow draped his thin shoulders. Wush didn't say anything. He just looked at her like she was a fool, lost dog who'd dragged herself home. He wore an apron that he tugged to the side. Then his eyes discovered Swede.

Andrea leaned against the door frame. "Wush, meet Swede," she said.

Swede shook Wush's hand vigorously.

"You brought your husband," Wush said.

"He's not my husband, Wush. I'm not married." She was deadpan. "He owns the new place," she said.

"I wish," said Swede. "I'm doing good to own my left big toe."

Wush didn't get it. He remained grim-faced. He said, "Never mind," as if he'd forgiven worse, and opened the door wide.

Andrea and Swede followed him into the kitchen. "What's this, Wush?" she said, because all his drawers hung open, showing Winnie's beaters, her scrapers, skinners, peelers, graters, mixers, and mashers; almost everything was out.

"Well," Wush said. He pulled up his trousers at the waist. He retucked his shirt. It was red like the door. "I'm cooking." He let his eyes wander over the kitchen drawers. "Where do you think she kept the measuring cups?" he finally said. "I've looked everywhere." He shoved his hands in his pockets and stared up high to the top shelf, to a row of green liqueur glasses.

"Top drawer," Andrea said. "Behind the silverware."

"Are we cooking?" said Swede. "I'm so hungry, I could graze."

Wush got on a footstool and peered in the cupboard with wide, confused eyes. Andrea dug behind the silverware and pulled out the set of yellow plastic measuring cups that nested each inside the next.

Wush was still poised, nose toward the cupboard. He lowered his arms and, hiking up his trousers, turned back toward the room. "Measuring cups," Andrea said.

Wush's eyes shifted to the cups. He focused on them for a while. Andrea knew if she swung the cups, Wush's eyes would follow.

Wush grabbed at a dented flour sifter.

"I can get the high things," said Swede.

Andrea glared at him. Wush nodded. Neither Swede nor Andrea seemed to be on his mind any longer, not even when the sifter appeared in Swede's hands.

"What are we making?" asked Swede.

Wush didn't answer. He pressed his lips tight in thought. "Somebody scald the milk," Wush said.

Swede two-stepped to the refrigerator and produced a pitcher of milk. He looked very pleased with himself.

"What do you want here?" Andrea whispered when Wush's back was turned. But he didn't hear. He was concentrating.

"How do you scald milk?" he asked, but Wush only handed him a pan.

"She put it up to there," Wush said. He touched a spot on the side of the pan. Swede put it up to there. "What do you think?" Wush picked up a bowl of froth and held it under Swede's nose. "This look right?"

"Yeast?" Swede asked. Couldn't he see, Andrea thought, that Wush did not answer questions? "Great," Swede said. "It looks great."

"Medium," Wush said. He twisted the temperature-control knob for the front burner.

Swede dropped the pan on the stove, and they heated the milk to boiling. Then they stood over the hot milk as it cooled, dipping their fingers in, in turn, to check the temperature, as if they were about to feed a baby.

"My father wouldn't row across the crick for nothing," Wush said. "My father wouldn't even row across the crick for a loaf of bread. But Winnie . . . Winnie made hot cross buns on Good Friday no matter what it took."

Swede nodded.

Wush tested the milk. "Time," he said.

"You got anything else to put in?" asked Swede.

"All we need's flour," said Wush. He rooted through the bread saver and held up a box.

"That's Bisquick," said Andrea, finally feeling useful.

"It's not flour?"

Andrea shook her head.

"All we got," said Wush.

"Well," Andrea said, "it'll save on rising time."

"Winnie gave them an hour in the sun."

Andrea shook her head again. "Twenty minutes in the oven. I know about Bisquick."

When the milk was cool, they poured it all together

with the yeast, beat it up, rolled it out, and cut out biscuits, though the dough was a little gooey.

Swede made the icing while the buns baked. Wush stood watching and smiling. They both saw the concentration in Wush's eyes and let the time slip by while the cottage toasted through in the heavy, earthy smell of yeast and baking bread.

The sun was up solid. Andrea sat on the porch in a ray of sun the way cats do.

"Nice old guy," Swede said, coming out. "I don't know any old guys. There was always rumors. I heard people got old. There's a rumor I have grandparents." They watched Wush pass from window to window, letting in the light. "I think they're in West Palm Beach. My dad's a fast burner, and somehow we sort of lost track."

"You can't lose track of your family," she said.

"You wanna bet?"

Wush came. He sat on his red kitchen chair that, come spring, became his red porch chair. They watched the herons feed and heard fishermen rev their motors in the boat yard.

"They're not burning, are they, son?" Wush asked. He'd settled back and, in the brightness of the morning, let his eyes close. Swede and Andrea went to the kitchen, where they found the buns were very done, low and wide and dark and done. They'd kind of stretched beyond the capacity of the flour.

Swede painted a wide cross on the tops of every stretched-low bun, and they put them on one of Winnie's platters.

"I split open my lieutenant's lip," Swede said. "He was an ass."

"You need help," she said.

Swede went out the door and came back with Wush's straw hat on his head. The polka-dot ribbon bobbed against his shoulder blade. Andrea watched it when she followed him back to the porch with the tray of buns.

"He's a real clown," Andrea said to Wush.

"How's this for a Panama hat?" he said to her. Now he wore a Panama hat and owl-eye reflector specs.

Wush and Swede and Andrea ate the hot cross buns. Icing drizzled down their chins.

"More like biscuits," mumbled Swede. The bread and sugar warmed Andrea's hands and her cheeks and her belly.

"They're buns," Wush mumbled back. "Hot cross buns."

Swede ate seven buns, as if he were half-starved. They must have warmed him, too, Andrea thought, after his nightmares in the cold night while he was slung in a hammock.

They both looked over at Wush. The sun had made his eyes too heavy, and he was sound asleep with his mouth open a little. Swede said, "I'm not going back."

41

# CHAPTER 5

# POPPER

ANDREA WANTED TO TELL SWEDE about her baby girl. She had touched her mother's face but never been invited to talk to her mother about anything that happened those three months. It surprised her how badly she wanted to tell Swede. She almost blurted out something on her way home from Wush's and found herself chewing up and down her fingernails, she was so on the verge of telling him things she didn't especially want him to know.

But she thought, No. He would find it a little disgusting, the way the kids in school did. He would be different and he would take off the straw hat Wush had said he could wear when they left.

Now she was home and Swede was on his roof. She could hear the hammering. She tried to think about the English exam on Monday. She could be studying *Moby Dick,* as Polly and Jen had sort of been doing. Andrea had been trying to read it for two months and the ship hadn't even left Nantucket. They weren't anywhere near meeting a whale. She wondered if they had the movie at Island Video.

Then she sketched a string of cartoon kids with *O*'s for mouths, and they looked back at her with surprise. Swede kept on hammering. She decided she was too fat. She didn't know what she was too fat for. But her waist clearly wasn't skinny, and she couldn't wear skintight jeans like her friends. She was meaty around the middle. She drew another chain of stick kids on stick skateboards. That would be her next shirt design. They sold to grandparents. They would say SUM SUM SUMMERTIME, or something equally hokey. She got up and stood at her mirror and brushed her hair and tried to braid it like the woman's at the ticket office. It was a French braid, and she worked her hair patiently, gathering up strand after strand until she had a good, if a little too loose, braid to the nape of her neck. She used to buy a cream to try to bleach her freckles, but looking at her freckles now, they didn't seem worth fighting. An idea about her baby crossed her mind; she wondered if her little girl would have freckles like her own, and if she did, Andrea could have told her not to bother with the bleach. There was a lot worse than freckles.

Bess was baking. The smell drifted up. Banana bread.

"Are you going to see Popper or am I?" Bess said when Andrea went downstairs.

"I am," Andrea said.

"Doesn't look like it."

"I just forgot. I went to see Wush."

"Don't fiddle with the bread."

"I'm not. I was just tasting."

"If you keep on tasting, you're not ever going to lose that weight."

Andrea looked at her mother. Bess looked suspiciously as though she were fiddling with the dish towel. That was close. She nearly hit on the subject of having babies, even though she seemed to kind of back into it, keeping herself protected by her durable, double-knit, all but bullet-proof pants. "Oh, he'd like some custard, too," Bess said. "And don't forget to see if the kitchen has any egg cartons for us."

She filled a small cup with baked custard and counted three wrapped butterscotch candies into a plastic bag. Her mother's hands were deft machines at needlework, husking corn, taking Communion, taking out splinters. They were fast and unflinching. She brought the knife down quick on her banana bread and cut Popper two inside slices and put them in another plastic bag that steamed up with their warmth. She packed them in a brown bag and handed that to Andrea.

"I'll go in a minute," Andrea said.

"You'll run into their lunchtime if you don't go now. The nurses' aides get annoyed if you're there during lunch."

44

"I won't get in the way, Mom."

"He didn't sleep in his bed," Bess said.

"Who didn't?"

"You know who."

"You mean Swede?"

Bess just pursed her lips.

"He slept by his house. Maybe he likes sleeping under the stars or something. Maybe the Army does that to you."

"That's ridiculous, Andrea. It was hardly thirty degrees last night."

Andrea shrugged.

"You mind your own business when it comes to him."

Andrea dug through a box of her watercolors for a picture she'd done for Popper and rolled it into a tube.

"I'm gonna go, Mom." Andrea took the bag.

Clint pulled up in his custom pickup, which was nothing like Sterling's. He had a sweating, ruddy face and a pipe between his teeth. Andrea went out as he came in. "I'd take him on any day." Clint liked to enter a room talking, as Sterling did. "That kid up there, nearly got the roof done."

Andrea followed the sound of the hammering down the bayberry path, through the oaks.

Swede came down when he saw her. He said, "I thought it might have more roof, you know? I thought I could live in it."

"For how long?" Andrea said. "How long do you have?"

"I don't know," he said. He pulled off a purple handkerchief he used for a sweatband. His eyes were bright blue. "I never did this before. But I thought it'd be nice to have a roof."

"Does anybody know you're here?"

"No."

"You made up all that stuff about checking on the work?"

"Well, yeah, but . . ."

"Isn't that desertion?"

"Not for sixty days. What are you, the judge?"

"What if your friends call your house and say you deserted?"

"Why don't you ask me, what if I starve here? Which is a whole lot more likely."

Andrea shook her head. "I came to ask if you want to go to Baytown with me."

"Sure," he said.

"To see my grandfather."

"Do we have to cook more Bisquick buns?" Swede said.

"Popper's in a nursing home," Andrea said. "He had a stroke."

Swede went to get his hat. "I don't mind cooking," Swede said.

"Just be quiet and wait here for me," she said. "I'd never hear the end of it if they knew."

Andrea screeched over the island's blacktop roads to the ferry in the Taggs' old Ford Valiant. With her was Swede and a mesh bag of treats and soap and odds and ends for Popper. Swede carried the bag and Andrea carried the watercolor she'd done of the creek. At the nursing home, Popper shook Swede's hand more welcomingly than any Tagg so far.

Popper smiled while they put him in a wheelchair. He smiled as they wheeled down the hall past frail women in their beds. One woman called, "Supper in ten minutes. Why does he always start his chores when I'm about to put supper on the table?" She spoke to Swede. Swede shook his head and held both hands up in surrender. Orderlies stood back for the two teenagers to shepherd Popper Tagg around the halls. Andrea pushed the chair and nodded at the women in their beds. She knew them all by name. They were a small parade down the corridors, over the black-and-white squares of scrubbed linoleum. Despite the cleanliness, the smell of urine seeped through the cracks and the walls. It was stronger than the pine disinfectant they used to clean, or cooking smells from the kitchen.

A woman in pretty lavender joined them, and she touched Popper's bald crown gently, a wifely touch.

"Ever seen the likes of it?" Popper said. "Where were all these girls when I was young?"

"A regular harem, Popper," Andrea said. She let Swede push the chair, and she put her arm through the arm of the woman in lavender and made her part of their parade. Swede drove the chair one-handed and carried the mesh bag over his shoulder like Santa. Andrea stopped at a lounge in the front of the house where the smell of urine was strongest, but it had tall windows to look over the harbor.

47

Popper looked out. He sat up straight, watching a crew scrape the bottom of a trawler. "No scallops this winter?"

"No, Popper, I told you. Another no-show."

Popper couldn't take his eyes off the pier. "Clams're all that withstood the brown tide."

"I know, Popper. Swede, here, is building on the island."

Popper's eyes flashed to Swede and back to the pier. "What'd you bring me?" he asked.

Andrea unloaded their packages and gave him the bag of banana bread.

"How goes it, Popper?" she asked.

"Good," he said. "Only my dreams . . . my dreams are like real life. I wake up and I know I've been across the crick with that old mule. I can smell that mule and I can smell them old bunker fish we plowed in." Popper took a bite of banana bread. "I wake up sore in the joints from pushing that plow. One time I was skating. I remember how we used to tie our skates on in the kitchen and go down t' the crick. We'd skate out to the bay and open up our jackets like sails and let the wind fly us clear back down the channel. I used to love that. Never know what I'm going to do in my dreams. More 'n once they have to pick me up off the floor."

Andrea put her hand on Popper's. His veins stuck out. "Tell Swede about the bands. I like it when you tell about the big bands that came to the hotel."

"Nothing to tell. Just heard the drums on a breezy summer night from the big hotels. Bongos." Popper grinned. "I used to love to hear them."

48

Popper put the last bit of bread in his mouth whole; a big grin curved over it as he chewed. "It's a great life if you don't weaken," he said.

Afterward Andrea and Swede went to a tourist deli called Spite Malice. On the walls were blown-up photos of ladies in black taffeta. Neither of them was very hungry after the nursing home, with all the hands reaching out and the smell. Swede ordered them raspberry fizzy drinks. They came in tall, elegant glasses from a tall, elegant waitress who Andrea figured must be biding her time until her break in the movies.

Andrea had been there once with a gang of girlfriends. It was another world, having girlfriends, and again she wanted to tell him about her baby girl.

"Two old guys in one day," Swede said. "You're related to more people than I've got in my company."

"They're not all related. It just feels like it. I feel related to Polly."

"Who's that?"

"Just a girl I know. We used to do everything together. Once I made us matching shorts and halter tops." Andrea shook her head, remembering. "Jeez, were we ever cool. Thirteen years old, and we were the last word on sex."

Swede leaned over his folded arms and peered up at her with his sunglasses propped on his peach-fuzz head. The straw hat hung down his back on the ribbons. "Great," he said very softly. "I'm fresh out of a tank with a squad of

guys, no kidding, all dressed up and no place to go. Dudes
with Musk cologne on so thick, you can't breathe."

Andrea started to laugh, imagining a tankful of guys
swabbed in Musk.

"Super," Swede said. "I'm glad this is so much fun for
you. I'm a deserter, and you're real concerned."

"I'm concerned," she said, but she couldn't stop laughing.

"All right, so just go on about you and Polly."

"Do they all wear hats like that?" Andrea said, tears of
laughter rolling down her cheeks. "In the tank? When they
put on their Musk?"

"You were saying how you learned about sex."

"We made it up," she said, wiping tears off her ears and
chin. "We were only thirteen. We knew everything. I've
still got that outfit. I outlined the shorts in yellow rickrack
and we wore them to the Firemen's Fair. That was the year
of 'Born in the U.S.A.,' and the firemen blasted that tape
all day and into the night. We could still hear it when we
got back to the crick and Polly and I smeared Noxzema on
each other's sunburn. And we ate corn tamales and we
could smell beer when the firemen danced with us. And
the Ferris wheel. We thought we could see the world
when we were on top of that Ferris wheel."

"About the opposite of a tank," Swede said.

It had started to rain. It made a swishing sound against
the window.

Swede talked about his nights with the men in his
squad, nights at the E Club. He told about going to

McDonald's for breakfast and watching the girls. "They're always Texas girls who get married to Army boys and they drawl," he told her. "That's what girls do who marry soldiers. They get jobs at McDonald's all over the world."

They traded stories. They had each other hooting and howling like two kids who had known each other a long time, like they had run around without shirts when they were toddlers and lay on their bellies, kicking the surf, like it couldn't spoil it that one was a girl and the other a boy.

"I'd like to see a tank," she said.

"No you wouldn't."

The laughing stopped, but it had loosened them up and made their minds sharp. The world seemed more describable.

"See, we had an exercise," Swede said. "The lieutenant said, 'Okay, you go that-away,' and in his game plan we get blown up. These other dudes come with stretchers and they haul us out of the tank and take us to a field hospital. And they tag us, so when a nurse takes a look at me, she sticks me off in a corner—like I'm not going to make it through the night. She doesn't pretend to put an IV in me. She doesn't give me nothing.

"Then along comes another guy with a tag that says I'm dead. I mean, they already took away everything else. You're already scum. Now you're dead scum. So on the way to Graves Registration, I see my CO. He's maybe twenty-two and already a lifer. And I hate the sight of his kinda pretty, heart-shaped face. I get up from being dead and ram my knuckles into his lip and cover him with his blood.

"And he says, 'What'd you do that for, Stuhr?' real hurt, like he thought I adored him. And then I skip Graves Registration and go on out the gate."

Andrea watched him while he talked. Then she began looking around the deli for goons, muscle-bound, armed soldiers.

"So you came here to a house with no roof."

"At least I'm not dead."

"I have to go home or I'm *going* to be dead."

"How old are you?" he asked.

"I just turned sixteen." It occurred to her that Polly would have said "almost seventeen." But Andrea was hanging on tight not to lose sixteen. "How old are you?"

"Nineteen," he said. He didn't say "almost twenty."

Before they could leave, the elegant waitress came to say if they weren't dining, they'd have to give up their table because it was rush hour, in case they hadn't noticed.

Andrea pulled Sterling's jacket tight around her, and they walked out into a black dusk and blowing rain and the heavy smell of salt and lobster and winter perch from the fish market. They didn't rush. They ambled past the tourist shops on the way back to the ferry and let the rain wash their faces.

It was a rough crossing. It was so rough that when they approached the boat, the ferrymen were hauling down on the lines to bring the ramp in nearly even with the dock.

The ferry was pitching, even anchored, in the slip. The men waved to Andrea to come on, then off, then to come on again, and Andrea said, "The hell with them," and she made a run for it the next time the ferry pitched forward.

"That was a fool stunt," one of the men hollered at her.

Andrea rolled down her window. "If I waited for you to get your act together, we'd never get home. You know, some people have places they have to *be*."

And Swede said, "That's it, get them real mad so they'll dump the car overboard, why don't you."

Theirs was the last car the men let on. Andrea got out and slammed the door while the ferrymen hauled up the ramp. Swede got out, and they wound their soggy way between cars to the rail, where they clung, two crazy, dripping people. The ferry kept heaving, and the bay pitched cold salt spray in their faces.

# CHAPTER 6

# ESTHER'S CREPERIE

SWEDE SAID HE'D JUST AS soon not come for supper because he didn't want the Taggs to slaughter any more family pets. They stopped by the island market and Swede stocked up on crackers and beefy noodles in foil pouches. Andrea drove the long way through the center in order to be able to drop him off before she came to her house. It was still raining hard, and Swede ran into the corner of the house with plywood over the roof beams. It was dank and cold, but the smell of spring rain and wet pine made it almost a haven.

She went into her own kitchen so wet, she left puddles at the door while she hung up Sterling's jacket. She

54

wrung out her hair in the sink, her head bent to the side. She felt a tiny bit pretty. She closed her eyes and ran her fingers through her hair to air-dry it and to re-member what it felt like to want to be gorgeous, and to pretend to be gorgeous. She and Polly had had as much fun pretending as any in-the-flesh gorgeous girl could have had.

"You're in trouble," Eleanore said.

Andrea opened her eyes and saw Eleanore on the floor with an ugly creature she was stitching.

"I'm always in trouble. What's that?"

"A potato person," Eleanore said. It looked to Andrea like the foot of one of Bess's support stockings stuffed with tissues. Eleanore ran a needle through, making tucks in the potato.

"What'd I do?" Andrea said.

"Nobody knows for sure," Eleanore said.

Bess came in the kitchen to check the meat loaf in the oven. She didn't look at Andrea. "Is the boy home?" she said.

"I don't know."

"Where have you been?"

"You know where, Mom. To Popper's. He ate all your bread."

Bess set meat loaf and potatoes on the table while Andrea laid out plates.

"He's not eating here?" Bess said, noticing she had only four plates.

Andrea said, "How should I know?" She couldn't stay.

55

She ran up to her room saying she had studying she had to do. From the bottom of the stairs Bess called, "Andrea, I don't know why you always think I was born yesterday."

Andrea felt filthy. She was a filthy and disgusting girl. She could hear it in the tone of her mother's voice.

She was hungry. She thought of Swede under the corner of his roof. At least she wasn't damp all the way through anymore, like he would still be. He would have stretched his sleeping bag on the new pine floor. She lay on her bed with *Moby Dick* because she did have to study. She held the paperback and turned the pages. Then she held the paperback upside down and turned the pages and the book was somewhat better.

She went into her parents' room and dug her baby book out of her mother's bottom drawer, from underneath her crocheted doilies and embroidered dresser scarves. She ripped out the picture of the tiny baby in Sterling's arms, herself, and the four-month-old wearing Sterling's watch cap and the one-year-old up to her elbows in birthday cake with dark-eyed Bess, who was almost smiling. She ripped out all her baby pictures and, with her mother's sewing sheers, diced them into stiff confetti.

Andrea woke up knowing the goons were coming in some shape or form. Maybe they were crossing the bay that minute and they soon would be bearing down on her road. It was Saturday; Esther would expect her at the store where she helped out and took her shirts and paintings to sell. She had five shirts. Sterling let her take the Valiant on Saturdays. It was early and she would go before they could stop her. She felt more starved than the screeching gulls could have been, but she wanted to get out of the house more than to eat. She hoped the kitchen would be empty and she'd sneak something as she passed through.

But when she got downstairs, she found Swede and Bess in earnest conversation. Bess was beating muffin batter. Swede had spun a chair around and folded his arms over the back. He put his square chin over his arms and leaned toward Bess, telling her about the Army.

He told funny stories about the guys, but he could not get a grin out of Bess. She dropped two heaping spoonfuls of batter into the muffin pan for each muffin and each time gave the spoon a lick with her finger.

"I think you are an immature young man," Bess said.

"People have told me that," he said, shaking his head. He winked at Andrea and snuck a gob of batter between Bess's machinelike motions.

Bess said, "My brother died in Vietnam, and the Army was nothing to crack jokes about. Not when people died. My brother's name is on the plaque up to the Legion Hall." Bess shut the muffins up tight in her 375-degree oven.

Swede unwound his legs from Bess's chair and stood up. He put on his sunglasses and the Panama hat. "The house is coming along great, Mrs. Tagg," he said, easing toward the door. He bowed, holding on to his hat. Andrea stuffed her painted shirts in a Woolworth's bag and Swede followed her out the door. Bess didn't stop them. But Andrea knew she would be mad and thinking Army leave can't last. There must be a war somewhere. Yes, she thought, he had stumbled into one.

"I hoped she'd give me a muffin," Swede said.

Andrea shook her head. "No, she was taking them to the Senior Center." She looked at him. "At least nobody came for you in the night."

"Maybe nobody missed me," he said. "Maybe they're less careful counting the dead."

"I don't know," said Andrea, as if that was something she might have known. He took off his sunglasses. He had tired eyes. His fuzz seemed to have grown a little in the night. He had nicked his chin shaving. It must have been cold, shaving from Clint's spout. The sun was streaming over them and the sea-hawk family was very shrill.

"Want to come to Esther's?" Andrea said. "It's sort of my morning job."

But Swede was already coming. He did not seem to want to get too far from her. He trudged beside her, looking at the weeds and gravel.

"I don't know what I can do for you," she said. She almost said, "I just had a little baby girl but I never saw her." Andrea thought what Swede thought, that she would seem less dead if she told that to somebody.

Instead she talked about flunking out. Swede got in the Valiant and laid his head back to soak up the sun. "I got

myself off the hook for a week in geometry," she said. "I
don't know anything about geometry, but I made this
spectacular geometric star with a hundred and fifty-two
straws. The teacher said we could do an extra-credit pro-
ject, and since I have about a sixty average, I needed that. I
like to make things, you know, fiddle with things. So I
made this with all acute angles. The star was as big as the
tar kettle up to the Legion Hall."

Andrea didn't know how the next thing happened. It
happened fast, she knew that. She had driven all the way
to Esther's store without stopping. She turned into the
parking lot, made a U-turn by the Presbyterian Church
graveyard, and, at the front door of the store, slammed
into a parked car.

"Great," Swede said pretty calmly. "I'm wanted by the
Army, and now the county sheriff."

Andrea put the car in reverse and backed away, leaving
the Volvo they had hit like a fresh kill under a sign that
read ESTHER'S CREPERIE. She got out and circled it.
Above the left front tire was a foot-long bruise smeared
with red from their Valiant. Andrea bent down and
touched it and looked at her fingers, as if she half expected
blood to come off on them. She was shaking.

Andrea's neighbor, Mr. Tocci, from around the point at
the mouth of the creek, came with a *New York Times* under
his arm. He saw his car. He saw their red car back off. He
didn't look at Andrea. "Idiots," he hissed. "You idiots."
He walked around it, too, as Andrea had done. "Just give
me your papers. Goddammit, it's brand-new."

"It's nothing but a scratch," Andrea said. "You can drive it. Why don't you go get your hemorrhoids fixed?" She said the last under her breath. Tocci finally glanced at her. They were not just gray-flannel sweats this guy was wearing, Andrea saw. They were designer sweats. He put his newspaper on his front seat. The Volvo reeked of fine leather. It clashed badly with the background of her family's graves, like Swede's house did with the chicken shed.

In a leather binder Tocci wrote down her license-plate number.

"Just call me up," Andrea said. "You don't have to go through all this."

Tocci ignored her.

"Look, I don't know what you're making such a big deal about."

He got inside his leather interior. Andrea grabbed the first thing she could find to write on, which was Swede's palm, because he offered it, and she copied down Tocci's license number as he swung past her church. "Have your goddamn lawyer call goddamn mine," she yelled, but he had turned on his tape deck and disappeared in a cloud of acoustic guitar.

"You should have hit the stone wall instead," Swede suggested.

"No," said Andrea. "That guy needed it." She patted the Valiant's hood. Her hands shook so bad, she couldn't trace the streak of Volvo silver across the red.

60

"I bet Bess says you're immature," Swede said. "And does she say you're not responsible?"

"She says that."

Swede and Andrea sat on the stone wall at the graveyard and watched the Easter weekenders come and go with their *Times*es and *Daily News*es and bear-claw pastries and bagels.

"You take responsibility," Swede said. "You got the guy's license. We'll turn him in for blocking the lot."

Andrea looked at him to see if he was real. In all her experience she had never come busting out of one of her stunts feeling this good. She thought about that.

"Yeah, I do," she said. "And I take responsibility for this not turning into a creperie," she told Swede, and pointed at the sign, ESTHER'S CREPERIE, blowing in the breeze. "It's true," she said. "When Esther bought the store, she hung up that wood engraving on those brass chains. But people worried because they didn't want crepes. They wanted to pick up a newspaper and get a cup of coffee, and that's what I told Esther. No one ripped the sign down, but they didn't pay any attention to it either. It's still like the old Center Store because Esther didn't push the crepes and the regulars kept coming."

"I could eat a crepe," he said. "I could eat those T-shirts."

"Come on," she said.

Andrea picked up one of a stack of newspapers outside the door to the store and Swede picked up another, and

Andrea didn't care if everybody in the store looked good and hard at her with this boy they'd never set eyes on.

It was busy at Esther's at eight o'clock. It was probably the busiest place on the island. The people eating at Esther's counter—the men with beer bellies and the girls she knew who spent their spare time cleaning and doing jobs for the rich people—turned to have a look at her and Swede. Esther's store smelled like butter and maple syrup and frying bacon.

"Did you see what that jerk did to me?" Andrea said.

Between trips to haul in papers, she told the story of Tocci's Volvo to road crews and truck drivers and girls in jeans with smocks that read MERRY MAIDS. Polly was one of them, too. Polly had gotten a job with the Merry Maids.

"So, Andrea, who'd you smash up?" yelled Polly across the store.

"I didn't smash up anybody," she yelled back. "I wish I had."

"Morning," Esther sang out to Andrea and Swede. That was like Esther, Andrea thought. She was the only person in town who would be friendly to a stranger.

Esther was frying links, flipping eggs, grinding Colombian coffee beans, ringing up sales, and telling gossip to the high-school janitor in her low, melodic voice. "John came home for his supper and his wife was gone. The first he knew she didn't adore him. Can you imagine?"

"Poor son of a gun," said the janitor.

Esther's eyes narrowed in sympathy as ground coffee

spilled on the floor, giving the store a thick, pungent layer of coffee aroma. Esther stepped through the overflow. Her yellow runners made tracks of coffee grains back and forth in front of the grill. She served two plates of sunny-side-up eggs and golden home fries. She patted the janitor on the shoulder. "Her husband's a poor son of a gun," she agreed.

She winked at Andrea and Swede. Swede winked back. "The librarian," Esther explained to Swede, leaning across the counter as if this were a secret only for him. "She moved in with the mailman."

Andrea introduced Swede to Esther. She wanted to get Swede's story straight because otherwise Esther would have made it up, and she would tell it to the janitor and anybody else who sat at her counter. Gossip made Esther sparkle, and she repeated it with compassion, even if it was a little smutty.

Andrea worked some more on the papers and warmed up in the heat of the cooking and the coffee brewing and the islanders' talk-talk-talk. Esther set the tone and let everybody be whatever they were, including Swede, who had his heart set on eating. Esther gave him pancakes and watched him with motherly delight as he wolfed them. Polly was still there, picking at her breakfast. She was as skinny as ever. Andrea wanted to show her the shirts she brought in, but she seemed preoccupied.

Andrea gave Esther the five shirts to display with the souvenirs, and Esther gave Andrea a bundle of egg boxes for Bess. Polly looked up then. Andrea saw her sneaking looks in the mirror above the grill. She looked, but she didn't bother to come over.

"You haven't sold them hens yet?" an old-timer named Lester asked Andrea.

"No," Andrea said. "Why should we sell the hens? They lay good. They're happy where they are."

"Yeah, I bet they are. They got about a couple-hundred-thousand-dollar view of the creek," he said, and the people at the counter laughed.

# CHAPTER 7

# HERON
# BEACH

"SO THERE'S A LIBRARY HERE?" Swede asked.

"Yup, and running water and refrigerators," Andrea said.

"I want to see if they have a book."

"Why not," she said.

When they went, the library wasn't open yet. They walked around the school and the Legion Hall with the tar kettle that used to be a whaler's try-pot and then was a fisherman's kettle for tarring his nets and today was only a flowerpot. Somebody would come and tend its daffodils, and when the daffodils died, somebody would plant sweet peas to trail down its heavy iron sides.

In front was the boulder and the plaque engraved with the names of war dead and drowned fishermen. Andrea's uncle was there, as well as many others with her family's name.

Swede sat on the rock and said, "This book I'm looking for, you'd like it. It's about a bird. You're always watching the birds. I never saw so many goddamn birds as you've got here, so I thought you've got to have this book."

"I don't want a book," she said. "Don't wait around for Julie to open for my sake. I've already got a book. I hate it."

"You won't hate this one," he said.

She made a face.

"No, it's like a movie, reading this one."

"*Moby Dick,*" she said, "is like green, slimy quicksand."

"Oh, *Moby Dick,*" Swede said. "Let me tell you the truth about *Moby Dick*. Not a living soul has ever read it."

"Markworthy, the teacher who's gonna flunk me, did."

Swede shook his head. "No he didn't."

"And Polly read it."

"Liars," he said. "No one ever has. See, you only have to read two or three chapters. One in the beginning, one midway, and maybe the end. That's all Mr. Markworthy ever read."

"I almost believe you," she said.

Swede said, "It's a fact. *Moby Dick* . . . Herman Melville didn't even read *Moby Dick*. He sleep-wrote it." Andrea was bent over laughing. "He sleep-wrote it because even he was bored with scrimshaw. How many pages have you read?"

"Forty," she managed to say.

"Forty in a row?" he asked.

She nodded. She couldn't talk anymore for laughing.

He bent down and took her hand. Then he let go of it and took off his hat and retook her hand. "In a row," he repeated with hushed respect. "Forty-pages-in-a-row-of-*Moby-Dick*."

An idiotic feeling that Andrea was going to bawl came over her, and she got up to see if Julie's car had pulled in, if somehow they had missed her car, whose muffler was so worn that people could hear Julie coming from the turn at the supermarket. They hadn't, though.

"What are you doing in the Army, Swede?" Andrea said.

"I say that to myself every day," he answered. "No, it's my father," he said. "Like I told you, he thinks it's good for me. He thinks like the ads. It will make me a man."

"What did you want to do?"

"I don't know. I wanted to lifeguard down on the Platte River and think about it. I'd like to still be thinking about it."

They went back to Esther's to buy sunflower seeds. They sat on the library steps to eat them and think.

Julie finally came, wearing a long blue skirt and a hip-length baggy sweater. "Polly calls her campy," Andrea whispered while they gave Julie time to arrange her things. "She kicked me and Polly out for eating bananas in the stacks."

"I'm looking for a book," Swede told the librarian when she looked ready for business.

She glanced up from changing the date on her stamp.

"It's about a heron but I can't remember who wrote it."
Andrea came up beside him.

"Look," Julie said, "help me out. Give me the author or
the title. Every other question I get is from somebody who
doesn't know anything, and I'm supposed to read their
subconsciouses."

"No, it's famous," Swede said.

"I'm sure it is," the librarian said.

Andrea made tiny heron's *quawk, quawk* sounds behind
him.

"There's a girl and she lives in the woods with her
grandmother," Swede began.

"Red Riding Hood," Andrea said.

"Last summer this guy was in," Julie said, "and he told me
a whole plot about a steam shovel named Mary Ann, and I'm
supposed to come up with the name of that one, too."

"*Mike Mulligan*," Swede said.

"So, honestly," the librarian said. She stamped several
cards.

"It was set in Maine," Swede said. "And somebody goes
to visit the bird." Julie began flipping through bins of cards.

"Wait a minute. She's got three names." Swede pushed
up the sleeves of his striped shirt. He was getting somewhere. "Jewett," he shouted. "Sarah Orne Jewett! *A White
Heron*." He shook his head in amazement, as if at the librarian's prowess. The librarian raised her eyebrows.

"Sarah Orne Jewett," he said to Andrea. "Where's the
fiction?"

"I don't know. I just come to eat bananas."

But they found it. *"A White Heron,"* Andrea read slowly when Swede pulled out the book.

"Let's get out of here," he said. "Do you have a library card?"

"What do you think? Just put it under your shirt."

"Let's do one thing legal. Could you get a card?"

"You think she'd give me a card?"

"Why not?"

"She hates me."

"This is a democracy. It doesn't matter if she hates you. She has to give you a card."

Andrea slouched over to the librarian's desk. "Need a library card," she drawled.

Swede stood behind her.

"ID," the librarian said.

"I'm not buying booze," Andrea said.

"Policy requires that I verify your residence on the island."

"I've been a resident all my life, and my dad all his. Ask at Esther's. Go out in the street and ask anybody if the Taggs haven't always lived here. I've lived here a lot longer than you, I bet. Go on, Swede, see who's walking down the street. Ask any of them."

Julie dropped a card and a pen on the counter. Andrea printed in black letters:

TAGG, ANDREA
TAGG CRICK
MANHANSET ISLAND
LONG ISLAND
NEW YORK.

Julie flipped through the phone directory for show, to confirm this information. She gave Andrea *A White Heron* and did not seem to care if the book or the girl or the boy ever came back.

Swede remembered Andrea telling him about Heron Beach, and he wanted to go there with the book. Andrea humored him. If Swede wanted to read a bird book, that was his trouble. She drove to Heron Beach without hitting anything, and they sat on the grassy dunes and Swede said that one of their problems was that they both liked to antagonize people.

"You're worse than me," she said.

"You haven't seen anything," he said. "Around you I feel like . . . I don't know, you're kind of wholesome, kind of like a dairy maid."

She pinched her cheeks. "My round, rosy face?" She squinted into the sun, trying to imagine herself in ruffles, bringing in the cows, the same person her father had called a slut.

"You're crazy," she said.

He said, "I'm less crazy here."

They stretched out and looked at the outline of the daytime moon. She picked up *A White Heron*. "It's skinny," she said. "Maybe I can read it instead of *Moby Dick*."

"I don't see why not," Swede said.

She took off her jacket in the sunshine. He took the book and flipped through and kept on saying how it was like a movie.

"So read it," she said. "Read it out loud." She dug her legs and her arms and all of herself deeper into the sand. The sand was warmed by the sun. It was warmer than the air.

And Swede began to read. His voice was Midwestern slow and in a monotone that wasn't hard to listen to. It was kind of a drawled monotone and it almost made her smile just to listen to Swede talk. His voice played with the world and said, Come off it. She thought he didn't want to take the world completely seriously. But some things got to him. He liked that book.

It didn't take long to read, only about twenty minutes because it was only a story, he explained.

Andrea didn't move. Not even her eyelids. "Did you fall asleep?" Swede accused her.

She said, "Sure enough, it's a white bird. We should have invited Julie, in case somebody else asks about this bird in Maine."

"Did you see pictures?" Swede asked. "Was that a movie or not?"

Andrea began to laugh. She grabbed up her jacket and dropped it over her face and howled. "It sounds like you're asking, 'Did you come?'"

"You're the crazy one," he said. He was truly offended.

"It was super," she said, shaking her head, and shaking the jacket off her face. She pressed her lips over a laugh. "Super," she said. He had those furrows in his forehead.

Andrea got up. She wore her purple goat shirt. She rolled the cuffs of her jeans up to her knees and walked into the surf. She bent and dug up a shell, using her hands like a dog's paws. The shell was violet, and she stood and held it in her hand.

A car with out-of-state plates pulled up to the beach, and Andrea ran out of the surf. She didn't know what for, maybe to cover Swede with her jacket in case these were the armed goons.

But it was a girl who got out, leading a toddler in a New York Yankees T-shirt.

"I thought your number was up," Andrea said, standing between him and the new people.

They watched the girl and the toddler. The little kid sang "Fine, fine," to Andrea, to the gulls, to the boy, to a fiddler crab, as if they had all asked how he was. He squatted down in the beach pebbles. "Fine," he squealed. Andrea thought the yellow kimono she had bought was even tinier than this kid's miniature clothes. He made her imagine again how small babies were when they came.

Andrea looked back at Swede. He was looking at her. She pushed her hair off the shoulder of her gaudy purple shirt and they went back to the car.

# CHAPTER 8

# The Mortician

BESS WAS WEARING A CORDUROY jacket. Her hair was bunched up under her little-girl hair band. She was in the vegetable stand the Taggs set up in the spring when people started coming back to the island. Andrea noticed her mother there at the same time she noticed the car. She and Swede pulled into the driveway and she worried that her mother was right there to see them. But the strange car was there, and Bess did not seem interested in Andrea or Swede. Bess's head was bowed over her eggs and her fresh stock of suncatchers, the geometric designs she crocheted inside gold rings, all different like snowflakes. They had one in their kitchen window, and sun rays filtered through its curves and arcs and angles.

Bess must have heard them coming, but she didn't look up. Behind her bowed head was the bright blue sign Andrea had painted advertising strawberries and farm-fresh eggs.

"That car," Andrea said to Swede. They were walking toward Bess.

"What about it?" said Swede.

"I don't know whose it is."

Swede sucked in his waist and heaved out his chest in mock bravado.

"Who's inside, Mom?" Andrea asked.

"A real-estate man." Bess was busy arranging eggs in trays by size. She had a lot of small pullet eggs and she marked them the cheapest. "I told Sterling I could have gone into real estate to make some money," Bess said.

Andrea watched her thick, deft fingers drop eggs in the cardboard boxes. Bess hardly looked at Andrea or Swede. The hens strutted around her ankles and walked across her feet like cats with cupboard love, as Bess called it.

Bess clicked her tongue and started for home. Andrea and Swede followed her and they went by way of the porch with a bucket of clams by the door.

It was half past four, the time when Bess was usually putting potatoes on for supper. A man in a navy-blue suit sat in Sterling's overstuffed chair. Sterling sat on the edge of the couch.

"Who died?" Andrea said.

"Leave us alone," Sterling said. He didn't want to fight. Both her parents ignored Swede. Swede seemed to be the least of their problems. She looked at the man in the navy-blue suit. He smiled. A cemetery-plot smile. Plots and caskets and a perpetual mowing service.

"It's near suppertime, Dad," she said.

"Leave us alone," he repeated.

Bess sat across from the mortician and picked up her crocheting.

Andrea said, "I'll start supper. I'll put the potatoes on," she said to the mortician. Her voice shook. She didn't want him to do this, this man in the navy-blue suit who didn't look at her once and was about to take away the one sure thing she had. She liked her room. She liked her window. It had been Popper's room, and all his brothers', when they were boys. All her stuff was in it. All the things she was were in it, and all the things she used to be when she was little.

She glanced at Sterling. "Another goddamn new house," Sterling said to the man.

"More than one," said the mortician. "If we do this right."

They left and Andrea shut the kitchen door, but she could still hear the man's voice. "It looks like more than an acre on the water or with a view," he said.

"You count the land across the road, you get more 'n an acre," Sterling said. "The view's a little spotty since the barn went up."

That'd be Stuhrs' place, Andrea knew.

"Beautiful parcel, Mr. Tagg." They could hear the *click, click, click* of a calculator. "Look," he said, "this is your first offer. You may do better." They could hear Bess's crochet hook tap on the gold ring of the suncatcher.

"What's a person supposed to say? Who ever heard of this kind of money?" Sterling said. "Christ, what do you say when somebody gives you the moon?"

Andrea was flat out on the floor, looking into the crack under the door. "*Giving* him. Giving him shit," she hissed.

"The taxes are more than you can bear," the mortician reminded Sterling.

"Can't pay 'em," he agreed. "And the place is falling down."

That was true. The back porch steps squeaked and jiggled. Fireflies came through the rips in the screen. Horsehair plaster dusted their plates, and the fragile laths that shaped the rickety house stood exposed.

"Can't work twenty-four hours a day," Sterling said. "Can't keep up with it."

Andrea got up and turned on a light over the sink and lit two candles. They were strawberry candles, and soon the kitchen smelled like waxy strawberry and plaster.

"He wouldn't do it," Swede said. "He wouldn't really sell it."

"He kidded about unloading it," Andrea said. "But nobody ever offered to take it. Nobody had ever wanted a handyman's special."

She ran water in the sink and started peeling the potatoes. Swede came to the sink. He helped her peel all the potatoes there were. The water was icy cold. It made her fingers ache and she knew it must make Swede's ache, too. He put down his paring knife once to take her hand, and she couldn't tell whose fingers were coldest.

Swede stayed for supper that night, and nobody asked why. Nobody said much at all. There was only a spell of cracking and snapping of clamshells, swishing through water, the *chunk, clunk* of empty shells into Bess's usurped bread bowl. All of them but Andrea were cracking and chunking. Andrea wouldn't eat them. Sterling poured salt in his palm. He poured some on the fried potatoes and tossed what he didn't use over his shoulder.

Andrea listened to the clunk of the shells. "Where would we go?" she said. "This is where we live."

"Nonsense," Bess said, meaning she would not give in to sentimentality, and if she had a daughter who was going to, she could do that someplace else as well.

*Chunk-a-chunk.* Two shells heaved at once. Sterling's eyes, like worry stones, took on a glint.

"Did you sell it, Dad?" Andrea said. He didn't look at her. Andrea felt like she was nothing but noise. *Chunk.*

"About the last waterfront in the family," Bess said. She was gazing through the suncatcher's magic. Bess could wonder, Andrea thought, but don't let her catch anybody else at it.

Eleanore asked for the butter. Swede found it. Then she asked for more milk. Swede was the one who got up and got the carton from the refrigerator. Bess was still counting Taggs on the creek. Eleanore was smart, Andrea thought. She was going to pretend nothing happened until it happened.

She watched Eleanore put on a milk mustache and smack her lips. Eleanore was the same way when Andrea began to show. Eleanore was eight and knew the truth about Santa Claus and where babies came from. She didn't ask questions, but she watched. Andrea made her sit on the glider swing one night for a talk about her own belly and how she would live with other girls having babies. Eleanore had listened well. And that night and other nights before Andrea left, she sometimes came in and slept with Andrea, but they didn't say anything much about the baby.

"Eat," Sterling said to Andrea.

Andrea rearranged her food.

"I didn't say paint a still life. I said, Eat it. Eat them steamers."

Sterling cracked open one more piss-clam shell. The bread bowl in the center of the table was a mound of gray, empty shells.

"Eat everything on your plate," Sterling said. He leaned back and clasped his hands behind his head. "I spent the morning digging them." Everyone's lips except Andrea's were shiny with butter. "You used to could dig five bushels easy in a morning. Now you're lucky to bring in a mess for supper. Crick's not what it was." He scowled. He looked like the brown tide and the pollution from the Sunday sailors was rushing his heart and his lungs and lapping his face, and it stank.

78

Eleanore said to Swede, "I won the Easter bunny house."

Sterling was leaning back. "Eat the steamers," he said again to Andrea.

Eleanore said, "It's all marshmallow chicks and jelly beans and chocolate-covered graham crackers, and I won it out of all my class."

"I'm not eating flesh," Andrea said.

"Goddammit all to hell," roared Sterling. He looked around the table to find someone as struck as he was by his daughter's idiocy. "'I'm not eating flesh,'" he said, mimicking her. "We are almost shipped off to one of them city shelters for the homeless, and you're trying out a food fad." Sterling got up and dumped the empty shells in the metal trash can. Bess got up to wash the dishes and Andrea ran upstairs, leaving Swede and Eleanore at the table.

She went to Eleanore's room, where she laid into Eleanore's prize bunny house. It tasted good after she had gotten used to chewing hard, crusted frosting and old graham cracker. She dug M&Ms off the bunny's footpath. She ate the peaked roof.

"Andrea!" Eleanore said. She and Swede stood in the doorway, watching Andrea with her cheeks pouched out and her jaw laboring over frosting and marshmallow chicks as thick as mortar. She'd eaten through the roof. It looked like a dozen sheep had grazed on it.

"Andrea," Eleanore said again, and went to pick up the unstuck jelly beans her sister hadn't inhaled.

79

When Andrea looked up, Swede told her she had pink marshmallow on her chin.

"Oh, well." Eleanore sighed like an old woman and ate speckled chocolate robins' eggs. Swede said it was making him a little sick just to watch them, but he ate whatever they offered.

Andrea got up and leaned on Eleanore's yellow bed and counted six terns on a glide over the creek. "I'm going down to the beach," she said.

Eleanore took her pajamas out from under the pillow and told Swede he could put his there. "You were supposed to get my room," she said.

"I like to sleep in the rain," he explained solemnly. He kidded with Eleanore for a while, and Andrea walked slowly down the hall, hoping to hear him come, and he did. She wouldn't have asked him. They found Bess in the kitchen surrounded by a lifetime's worth of kitchen helpers, her egg slicers and flour sifters and more trivets than there were Taggs.

For one second Andrea thought of Winnie Huckins when she was real old. She used to paint her big hooked toenails purple and perch on her kitchen stool. From it she could open all her drawers and reach all her kitchen helpers and still cook the meals. For one second Bess was old and frail with purple, hooked toes, and it stopped Andrea short. But then Bess's machinelike fingers whipped a bit of hair off her forehead, and Andrea sashayed past her with Swede, making a display of opening the door.

They walked to Heron Beach. It was cold, and Andrea

80

wore only a T-shirt and jeans. He touched her shoulder, and his hand felt huge and warm. Swede wasn't much taller than she was, and as he began to grow actual hair, his jaw and eye sockets didn't seem so bony and cave-manlike. Or maybe she was only getting used to him. It had been awhile since she had been with anybody. That could account for the hugeness and the warmth. She was so cold.

They walked on a crescent of beach that circled the bay. Across it came a northerly wind that followed the sun-down. She was so cold that when she first felt the warmth of his hand, a shiver like lightning cut through her from her shoulders to her knees.

"Want to go someplace to warm up?" Swede said.

"No," she said.

The tide was out and they made deep tracks in the sand-bars off the beach.

"What's that? A puffin?" Swede asked.

In the moonlight Andrea could see a gull alone on a rock. "We don't have puffins," she said. "Puffins are in the Arctic. They don't get any farther south than someplace in Maine."

"Well," he said, "it looks enough like a puffin. They're all puffins to me."

Andrea tried to turn the gulls into squat black-and-white things with gaudy-orange beaks. She pointed out the top of a telephone pole beside the road. A wooden crossbar was fixed to the top. On that was a messy pile of sticks going every which way, like a beaver's dam.

"It's a fish hawk's nest," she said.

"That's the kind on my roof."

"Come on, I'll show you something farther down."

They walked soundlessly over the sand with the hollow shrieks of gulls as their music.

"Watch over there," she said, pointing to patches of grass growing in the sand. She stretched out on a flat rock on her belly. Swede stretched out beside her. "Now don't move," she whispered.

# CHAPTER 9

# LEAST TERN

HALF-HIDDEN IN THE SEA grass were white birds whose black wings were folded close to their bodies. There were five or six mounds of white, fringed in dark. They were near enough that she could imagine putting her palm on one and feeling its heart beat.

"They're sitting on sort of brownish spotted eggs," Andrea whispered.

"What are they?"

"Terns. This is about the only place on the island they nest. The gulls keep driving the terns off the beaches, but I've counted eighteen pair here."

A car's headlights flashed across them, then clicked off.

"Run," Andrea whispered loudly.

Swede's feet wedged between the rocks.

"This way." Andrea pulled at him, and they ran. She heard footsteps behind them and men's voices. They spoke in soft, urgent tones. But the footsteps broke into a run.

"Who are they after? You or me?" Swede called.

He pointed at her in the moonlight. She pointed at him. And they ran.

Andrea veered off toward the water. The men's breath came loud and labored, as if they were old or maybe too fat. Swede and Andrea ran silently across the sand.

"Your stripes!" Andrea hissed. "You look like an escapee." The stripes ran like they could have been running on their own. And they ran.

"You want to give me some clue about what we're doing?" he said. They had stopped at a rocky wall where they burrowed against the stones. Dry seaweed scratched Andrea's neck, and something sharp, maybe the shell of a horseshoe crab, dug into her thigh. Swede's hand gripped hers and she was aware of his heart pounding.

"It's the tern wardens," she said.

"The what?"

"Tern wardens. Kind of like vigilante groups to catch people messing around where they nest."

"What were we doing?"

"Just being here."

"Are you trying to scare the shit out of me?"

They were so close, she could feel his growing-out fuzz.

"Was that a rifle?" Andrea asked.

"I don't think so," he said.

"I wouldn't put it past them to have a rifle."

"They'll come back this way to their car," Swede said.

"Let's slit their tires," she said.

The men turned. Andrea tightened her muscles against the rocks. She burrowed into the seaweed. At that second all she wanted was not to be seen.

The men didn't see them. They passed together, in step, quick and angry. Beyond them was a telephone pole against the blue-black sky. That telephone pole had a platform, too, and a beaver-dam fish-hawk nest.

"They're always telling me to go," Andrea said. "I'm always telling them to shove it. It's my beach, too."

"Yeah," he said. "I've got the same sort of knack with people."

Swede and Andrea uncurled themselves from the rocks and each other.

She got up and roughly brushed sand off her jeans. She ran up the road toward the crescent where the terns nested.

"You call them puffins, and Popper calls them all sea swallows," she said. "That's 'cause they're delicate, not like the gulls. Look at how their beaks and their tails swoop up in a vee. I come here and stretch out on that rock and see what hatched. Some of them are stupid. Some of them nest in the flats, and when the tide is extra high, they don't make it. Those are the least terns. They're the smallest. They have yellow beaks, and when they fly, you can see their yellow feet."

85

They stretched out again and watched the pearly sea swallows rustle in the grass and some others farther out on the flats. The wind seemed gentler. The clouds settled and left the moon bare and white like a huge paper lantern.

She glanced at Swede. He was lying on his back, eyes wide open like somebody shot him.

"What are you thinking?"

"I'm thinking I got in a nest too far out on the flats. People keep giving you impossible choices. You want to lose out in the triage and go to Graves Registration, or you want to tear open your lieutenant's lip and hop a bus?"

"I want to tear open my lieutenant's lip," she said.

"And then you come to a desert island," he said, "and meet up with a girl who you like, and all you can think about is your lieutenant's blood. The guy had freckles on his lip, which you split. For all you know, the guy's also got your pay, and here you are without a buck. And on a three-year hitch, owing three goddamn years to a stupid freckle-lipped kid who's there now making a stack of your pay slips.

"So here's your next choice. Let a couple of militant birders turn you into a basket case or go back and ask nicely for another turn. You changed your mind. It was really swell."

Andrea had been watching the bell buoy bounce while he talked, and when he stopped, she kept on watching, only the world seemed as bare as the moon. "Tell me some more," she said. She didn't want him to stop talking. "Tell me about when you hit him."

Instead he came and took her in his arms, and she felt both their hearts beat along—*ratchety, ratchety*—like a couple of broken-down cars.

"And you're about to get kicked out of your house," he said.

"That's one thing," she said.

"All right, what else?"

"I just had a baby," she said. "A baby girl." She had said that before. She'd told Bess it was a girl. Bess had said she was very, very sorry, as if Andrea had survived a car wreck but the wounds were permanent. "And I miss her," Andrea said. She hadn't said that out loud to anybody.

Swede sat up and shoved the hair he barely had off his forehead. "Who's the guy?" he said. "Do you still go with the guy?"

Andrea shrugged. "It wasn't like that," she said. "Nothing like that."

"Where's the kid?"

"I had her in a special home and let her go for adoption."

"But why? If the guy didn't mean anything, why?"

"You mean, why didn't I get an abortion?"

"Yeah."

"I don't know," she said. "I would have. I wanted to. My parents wanted me to. I don't think it's bad. I know a girl who did it. She went on a Saturday morning and she came back across Saturday afternoon and she went home and her boyfriend brought over pizza and she was so happy. She said she just slept a lot but she was so happy. But I didn't do that."

"Was it your religion?"

"No. Well . . . maybe religion, but not like church. And not like any of those groups or those people who try to pass laws to tell you what to do. Not that at all. It was personal. It was just me and what was happening to me. See, I just waited too long. School was starting and everybody was getting, oh, you know, jean skirts and report folders, and I kept thinking this can't be happening to me. I waited *too* long. I felt her move. And I couldn't do it."

They were both on their backs, looking at the stars.

"The minister told Mom about a home upstate and I went there, so now it's over with."

They didn't talk for a long while. Then he sat up. "When?" he said.

"February sixth." Andrea faced him. "February sixth, 1:09 A.M. Six pounds, one-half ounce."

"Yellow hair like yours?"

"Don't fool yourself. Not a blond gene in my family."

They looked at each other with similar crooked grins on their faces.

"It was reddish, I think. Reddish brown. I didn't see it myself," Andrea said. "The nurse said I wouldn't stop thinking about her if I didn't see her once, but I didn't think that would help. The nurse said she looked great as far as newborns go."

Andrea watched the terns and waited to feel stupid for saying any of that. But she never did. Swede lay back down on his back like before with his eyes open, as if he'd been shot. She began to wonder if that was his natural pose. She listened to the surf.

After a while she said, "So, are you going back to the post?"

He said, "I don't know."

He tucked his arm under her and nestled her against him.

When they started to walk home, Andrea showed him a signpost by the road. It was very official and loomed taller than a traffic sign. It read:

---
WARNING
---

COLONIAL BIRD NESTING AREA
Federal laws prohibit the taking or molesting
of birds, their nests, eggs, or young. This could
subject eggs and young to exposure and possible

DEATH

"Never mind the birds," Andrea said. "The Taggs could use a sign like that."

# CHAPTER 10

# EASTER

THEY DECIDED THAT ON EASTER morning Swede would work on his roof and Andrea would work on *Moby Dick*. Or sometimes Andrea would work on the roof and Swede would read *Moby Dick* out loud.

Andrea found Swede hunkered down in his green nylon bag. The canvas tarp he'd strung between the trees smelled strong and good. It made Andrea feel as though they were in the wilderness, combating the elements and the odds.

The Presbyterian Church's bells rang. The wind blew "Ring Out, Wild Bells" down to the creek. Swede snorted. He rolled over on his back and his dog tags dangled out the zipper. He was so fair, his eyelashes were white. She didn't think he had worn the dog tags yesterday.

"I came to say you can have the bathroom if you want," she said. "They went to church."

Swede opened his eyes, but he didn't talk. He was always talking about one dumb thing or another, but now he just squinted at her.

"So do you want to come?"

"I could use a shower," he said.

Swede sang in the car but he didn't sing in the shower, at least not that morning. When he came out, he had on his disguise again, his sunglasses and his Panama hat. They scrambled eggs and ate Bess's homemade bread. Swede took a knife to a fresh loaf. He cut it into six hunks and called it Texas toast.

The kitchen looked the way it always looked, Andrea thought. Lived in, eaten in, painted in. It had Sterling's dirty socks and Eleanore's potato people and Bess's sun-catcher, catching rays of sun and dust. She gathered her things to study while Swede dug toast from between the toaster coils.

"How do you write an essay?" she asked.

"Three main points."

"Three main points," she repeated. She could do that, she thought. Her mind danced with possible points. Everything seemed possible. The sale of her house would fall through. Markworthy would pass her. Her T-shirts would become a national rage.

"Here's the future," she told Swede. "I'm going to become an entrepreneur. You will get a special discharge from the Army for meritorious service for having died.

And then," she said, "I'll open a restaurant and you can eat all the leftovers so we won't need a dog.

"And we'll be neighbors—you there, and me here, and you can lifeguard and think. I'll paint the least terns' yellow feet because I like seeing them fly with their yellow feet swinging free."

Swede chewed and nodded.

It made Andrea more determined. If he was going to be grim, she was going to be cheery.

Andrea wrapped her hair around her head and held it up. "Or," she said, "I'll run a living-history museum. I'll dress up, build a shack on the beach, and shuck scallops. Mr. Tocci will come and say, 'What a charming neighbor. What a scallop shucker! Won't you borrow my Volvo, or my yacht, or my small seaside mansion for parties?'"

Swede had eaten all the Texas toast. He wasn't in her silly mood, but he was still ravenous. He ate and now and then nodded, as if she were talking perfect sense. Since she'd found him asleep with his dog tags on, he hadn't been silly.

"And from the profits of recreating the true life of scalloping, I'll build on." She pointed up. "I'll build another floor and it will have a turret. My friends can paint pictures on the walls. They can fly kites from my turret."

She sat down and let go of her coiled hair. "And terns can sleep over," she finished, and so much seemed impossible.

Swede looked at his watch, and she knew that instead of nailing his roof he was probably going to go back to the post, which was the sensible thing to do.

"I was just thinking about that kid," Swede said. "The one you told me about."

"Yeah," Andrea said.

"Well, do you know where she is? Can you ever see her?"

Andrea was slipping into hating again. She was hating the Army. She was hating the lieutenant with the split lip, as she hated Markworthy and Sterling and Ms. Brock at the home who talked to Andrea like she was a stupid girl.

"The day after I got back to the island, I got a letter from the social worker, Ms. Brock. She said, 'The baby was placed in a good Christian home. She has an older brother and parents who love her.' That's it. That's what I know."

Swede rubbed crumbs off his smooth-shaved face.

"So are you leaving today," Andrea said, "or are you hammering?"

"I'm hammering," he said.

"Okay," she said.

They went off, walking with a purpose, like workmen to the mines.

To Andrea the worst thing about her book was that when she looked at it, she heard Markworthy booming. It was Markworthy's book. But she continued to look at it right side up, dabbing at lines here and there with a yellow highlighter as she swung herself in Swede's hammock.

After a while her parents must have come home because Eleanore came trudging through the bayberries. Andrea by then was on the roof, nailing down a sheet of plywood. Swede skipped a lot of pages and was reading about Queequeg building his coffin. Eleanore would listen to anything, and she sat down at the bottom of Andrea's ladder. Every time Queequeg did something odd, Eleanore said, "Is that true?"

"It's a story," Swede always said.

Andrea stopped hammering because she wanted to hear about Queequeg's drawings and the tattoos all over his body. "Read that part again about the riddle," Andrea said.

"'Queequeg in his own proper person was a riddle to unfold.'"

"What does it mean?" Eleanore said.

"See, the guy's covered in tattoos. He looks like a quilt with all these tiny squares and triangles drawn right on his skin."

"Like a sea turtle's shell?" Eleanore asked.

"Yeah, like a turtle," Andrea said. She thought of all the mysteries of the world being explained on the seaman's skin. She thought of her father with tattoos. For one second it was a little like an antidote to hate, to think how complex and mysterious a person was. Not to like or dislike, just to wonder.

"Mom's mad," Eleanore said. "And that's not a riddle."

"Why's Mom mad?" Andrea said.

"Somebody just called."

"Who called?" Andrea said patiently. "Was Aunt Tessa snotty again?"

"It was somebody from Nebraska," Eleanore said.

Swede wandered over to the ladder.

"She wasn't mad right away," Eleanore said. "She was kind of stiff, you know, not like when she talks to Aunt Tessa. They talked about weather in Nebraska."

"Yeah, so what happened?"

"At the end I knew she was mad."

"How?"

"I was listening."

"Since when do we have an extension?"

"No, I was listening to Mom. I can tell by the way she says 'mm-hmm.' I can tell when it's time to ask for something by the way she says 'mm-hmm' and 'Don't you know it?'"

"What do you think the other lady said?"

"They must have been talking about this house because Mom said, 'Clint thinks it will be done mid-June,' and then she said you were helping." She pointed at Swede.

"Oh, sh—" Andrea mouthed the word.

"See, I knew you were in trouble 'cause that surprised the lady. Then Mom had to tell her when Swede came and what he looked like. By this time Mom's real mad, and at the end she told the lady she had a heck of a lot more things to do than that. I didn't figure out what the lady wanted her to do."

Bess appeared on the road. She was quiet as a cat because she wore her sneakers. She wore gold loops in her ears and she had curled her hair for Easter. She stood square-footed on the blacktop road.

Andrea leaned against the pine frame of the house. Swede looked like he might bolt.

"I've done everything that's been done to that house by myself for twenty years. And now I'm doing everything myself to pack up and move us out of that house, and I've got so much on my hands that if he's AWOL"— she pointed toward Swede and glared at Andrea—"I don't want to know. And if you've got any sense, you won't tell Sterling. Where do you find them? How do you always find such strange boys? I have never seen his eyes. I couldn't even tell his mother what kind of eyes he has."

"The blue kind, ma'am," Swede said.

"Why is he wearing Wush's door decoration?" Bess asked.

"For shade," Andrea said.

Bess looked at the heavens and turned around cat-quiet to go home. "All hell's breaking loose, so what's one more thing? AWOL soldiers. Why not?"

"Then locusts," Swede suggested.

"Don't smart-mouth me. Your mother said call home, and that's all I'm saying."

Eleanore took it in from underneath the ladder, and then she ran back through the bayberries.

"I better go," Andrea said when her mother and Eleanore were gone.

He said, "What if the goons come?"

"I have to help her. People just bought up our only house to use as a summer spot when they're in the mood. Or they might raze it. Maybe it's too junky to live. Sorry," she said, and started to run toward the path.

96

Swede said he was coming.

"All right. Come on."

Andrea found out that the buyers wanted to take possession fast or they might change their minds. By the afternoon of Easter Sunday, they walked through corridors of Tagg possessions to get from the kitchen table to the cellar door.

Bess was hauling things down from the attic. Swede helped her carry dresses on thick wooden hangers. The dresses smelled like mothballs and reminded Andrea of goofy dress-up games with Polly. Then Swede carried down a wooden box of silverware that Bess had won at the Firemen's Fair when she was seventeen.

Sterling and Eleanore pounded up the cellar stairs, bringing cracked terra-cotta pots. They set them at Bess's feet and all but wagged their tails. Andrea could see they had already brought up two broken outboard motors, Popper's bottle collection in six soggy boxes, and a lot of garbage—all for Bess.

"I have no idea where we're going to put it," Bess said. "If you see anything you want, take it," she said to Swede. "On the walls, anywhere." She fluttered her fingers around the room. Eleanore said Swede should take the cross-stitch pictures for his barracks.

Swede went with Andrea to start on her room. She had an old-fashioned dressing table with a big oval mirror. She opened all its bulging drawers and tried to imagine where to begin. She picked up a fishbowl with a funny combination of things: rough stone arrowheads that were Popper's finds while he worked the land around the creek, lip glosses, condoms, mascara with little brushes to put it on with. There was also a wooden plaque strung on yarn. It read, FIRST PLACE—BEAUTY PAGEANT.

"The Firemen's Fair last year," she said, and dropped the plaque in her pocket.

"What about them?"

"The rubbers? They were free. We got tested at the home and lectured long enough to last till menopause.

"But the makeup wasn't. Once Polly and I joined this club," Andrea said. "They called it World of Beauty, and you could join by sending in this coupon we found in a magazine. And World of Beauty sent us a mess of stuff in a box. It opened like it was jewels, with pop-up rows of blush and bins of lip gloss and contour shading and eye shadow and these brushes to swirl it all around with. So here we are, me and Polly, sitting in the kitchen doing each other's faces. And here comes Dad, and I mean by the time he comes through, Gawd, are we beautiful.

"He says, 'What's this?' And I say, 'We joined World of Beauty.' And we open the bins and secret drawers and let him see all the colors. And we say 'Oooooo,' like we're showing him the queen's jewels.

"And he says, 'How much?'

"'Nothing,' we say, both together. 'They gave it free for a coupon.' And I'm looking up and Polly's got blue eyeliner under her eyes, and I made a little X at the corner for show and she did mine green. But when Dad asked, 'How much?' that's when I knew it wasn't free.

"It was money, and that's something. And Dad never had any. He knows about owing, and as soon as he saw the World of Beauty all over our kitchen table, he knew it didn't matter what the coupon said. It means we owe. And that's the story of our life, and here we are living where most people have sacks of gold.

"And in April, here comes this letter Mom brings home with the mail that says the World of Beauty had hired the International Credit Association. It says, PAST DUE. PAY NOW—$24.95."

"That's false advertising," Swede said. "You didn't have to pay it."

"That's not the way Dad saw it. I am still using the stuff," Andrea said, and came to show him her eyelids in proof. "The stuff's three years old. It cracks in the cold."

"What'd Sterling do?"

"Let's just say he hauls it up whenever he's making a point about my character."

# CHAPTER 11

# TATTOOS

SWEDE STAYED IN THE TAGGS' house that night, and no one seemed to notice. In the morning he made oatmeal for Eleanore while Bess was down cellar digging through the canning jars. Andrea ate jelly toast and put on makeup at the kitchen table. They heard the chink of the canning jars being jostled together. The sound traveled up the cellar stairs.

Since the phone call, Andrea thought she and Swede and maybe Bess knew something was about to happen. Swede had kidded and said the goons would come in tanks because he was so violent. There'd be a standoff from the rafters and then he'd swing down by a rope, something like Indiana Jones, and Andrea would repel from the deck. Andrea had said, "Good, at least we have a plan."

"Don't forget the Fifties Dance tonight," Bess called from the cellar.

Everybody went to the Fifties Dance. Sometimes Andrea thought the Fifties Dance was more like church than church. All ages went, and people put aside differences to dance to old rock and roll. The Taggs might be moving, and the tanks might be coming, but the Fifties Dance was a little bit of sin they allowed and counted on.

On top of it all, it was *Moby Dick* day. Her parents only knew about her schoolwork when she got *F*'s because *F*'s had to be signed. If she didn't get an *F,* they didn't know anything and didn't ask. That was her business. They had their own. *Moby Dick* was her business, and it had become the one thing she had the smallest control over.

She looked at Swede. He was scrubbing the oatmeal pot. "We could go to Esther's," she said.

"Both of you go," Bess said. She came to the top of the stairs. She still wore the gold loops in her ears to clean out the cellar. "You've been missing days, and you owe her. And ask around if anybody wants some hens. Go on—you can catch a ride with your father."

They rode three in a row in the front seat of Sterling's truck. Sterling hadn't shaved. He lit a cigarette and talked about how they'd build a little ranch house with built-in closets and a built-in dishwasher in the new subdivision.

At Esther's, Swede sat at the counter and ordered another breakfast. Andrea worked on the papers and listened to her father.

"Done," he said.

"What's that, Sterling?" asked a man from the boat yard.

"Signed the papers," Sterling said. "Sold the homestead and all the land."

"Bless your heart," Esther whispered, and looked at Andrea.

"Realtor subdivided like he said. Sold my place separate and gonna sell the upper lot separate. Said he'd get me double that way, and he wasn't kidding."

"So what'd you squeeze 'em for?"

"I'll get by," Sterling said.

Sterling was talking to Norm Wheeler, the janitor, who was telling about when they sold the Wheeler farm. Sterling held the butt of his cigarette in his fisted fingers. There was red-and-gray stubble on his chin and taut upper lip. His gaze never flinched. Andrea turned her back on the counter and pulled old papers out of the stacks on the wood floor.

Marie, one of the Merry Maids, came in. She sat at the counter, and he told her what he'd gotten for their house. The old men at the counter shook their heads and said they didn't know the world they were living in.

Marie wore a blue nylon smock like the girls in Woolworth's. She had dropped out when they offered her a fortune to shuttle around in a VW cleaning up after people. She cleaned her own house, the one her family sold. Her family had been farmers, too. Once Marie told Andrea that was the only way to stay on, by scrubbing people's johns.

Esther came bringing in a baking sheet of cinnamon rolls from the kitchen. Swede sat at the counter and ate pancakes and watched the door. Andrea tied a rough-clothed apron around herself and took the sheet of rolls from Esther, who was flying past in her yellow sneakers. Andrea leaned on her elbows and lazily spooned sugar glaze over the sweet brown bread.

When Polly came in, Andrea forced herself to keep drizzling on the glaze. She wanted to grab her by both arms and sit her down and make her talk. Polly bought a chocolate bar. She always bought a chocolate bar before school.

"You almost eat as much as him," Andrea called to her.

"Who?"

"Swede."

"You never introduced us."

"Swede," Andrea said, "this is Polly."

He nodded because his mouth was full.

"Are you moving?" asked Polly. "Esther said something about it."

Polly had short, shiny black hair. She worked very hard in school and did everything. She took pictures of people in outrageous poses for the yearbook. She played drums in the swing band. She didn't do it very well, but she did it very carefully.

"We're packing," Andrea told her. She drizzled frosting and looked at the design she created. If she looked at Polly, Polly might go away. "It's crazy," she said. "Everything's happening so fast. I feel like those people on the news who are running with carts of clothes and pots and pans, and you can hear gunfire in the background."

103

Polly laughed a little. Andrea didn't think she understood, or she had other things on her mind. All she said was, "So where are you moving?"

"Maybe to Aunt Tessa's for a while."

Polly laughed for real then. "Wow," she said. "That'll be a trip. At least you won't leave the island."

That was it? Andrea thought. She could have used some tears or some memories. They both had grown up there. But Polly didn't say anything else. She crammed the candy bar in her purse when the first school bell rang. They said good-bye to each other and she left.

Andrea went on frosting the rolls. Swede was right across the counter from her. "They go all out here," she said, "to show how much they care. Hallmark could get them to write greetings. They could write 'tough shit' over and over in the shape of a fish."

Swede said, "I just wondered. You didn't tell her much about that kid?"

"Not much. She wouldn't understand." She gave Swede a small, slightly twisted smile. "I mean, look at her. She's a virgin."

Swede shrugged.

Andrea decided she would work on turning Polly into a tattooed harpooner. She tried to tuck her away there to study her tattoos when she was up to it.

"Esta," Norm Wheeler called. "Esta, let's have a fill-up."

Esther filled his mug. She played soft rock on the radio, Carly Simon and James Taylor singing "Devoted to You."

Sterling left. Andrea licked the glaze off her fingers. She

unpeeled a roll and ate it half-moon by half-moon. She heard the second school bell.

Lester came to talk to Andrea. He was deaf, and he always yelled. "You shouldn't've sold off," he yelled at Andrea.

"We had to," Andrea yelled back. "They offered us the moon."

Andrea asked Lester if he wanted some hens. "I told Ma to put up a sign: FREE HENS TO GOOD HOMES." Lester clicked his teeth.

Andrea rolled up the sleeves of Sterling's jacket because it wasn't so cold, and she and Swede walked outside. They walked through the churchyard, among the old thin stones shaped like jigsaw puzzle pieces.

"I'm going to school," she said.

"Good," he said, not looking at her.

She shook her bangs out of her face.

"Maybe you can make one of those geometric stars for Markworthy."

"I'll go see," she said. "I better go before it's too late." She zigzagged away from him through the stones. Everybody would be talking about the Taggs in that school, she bet. Or maybe not. She didn't know which was worse. She would give them all tattoos.

"I'll hang around," he called. "I'll go see the librarian."

"Great, make her day," Andrea called back.

"Hey, Swede," she said softly. He was sound asleep at a kid's table in Julie's library.

"Andrea?" he whispered back. He rubbed his eyes.

"Early release," she said.

"Somebody's merciful."

"You hungry?" she asked.

"No."

Something was happening between them. Something was different. They started to talk in mumble words that were just for each other. It was natural to touch. It just happened. It wasn't embarrassing. It was a mutual need. It was nothing like the boy on the beach.

"You awake?" she said.

He moved his hands and looked at her. He took her hand and kissed the stars on her fingernails.

"You have the exam?" he asked.

"Yup."

"It was okay?"

"I don't know. I wrote things."

"Good."

She took her hand away. She wasn't sure why, but she was not going to let this happen. The day was warmer. She felt flushed and she pulled her hair back. "Look," she said, "I've got better things to do than sit at a little kid's table getting lovey."

"Right," Swede said. He raked his chair back.

"Esther said she'd give me a couple extra hours today if I wanted."

He didn't answer, and she didn't know how to explain.

She left him there, mad, and went back to Esther's, where a tour bus had pulled in and Esther's grill was hot and sizzling with burgers. Everybody passing from the north to the south fork seemed to have stopped at Esther's. Bright, flowered people in camp clothes and walking caps. All the people couldn't fit at the counter, so some of them held Styrofoam cups of coffee and browsed. They looked at Andrea's note cards with watercolors of the ferry and delicate terns and her crazy T-shirts.

That's when the idea came to her about starting from scratch.

It seemed like everything that she touched or let touch her, she held on to for dear life. She had to stop that, because if she touched it, she seemed to be losing it for sure. The baby for one, even if she didn't want to be a mother. What could she do for a baby? Andrea thought the baby might be better off with a regular brother and regular parents. But the baby touched her, and she couldn't let go.

And now all the hustle and packing at home meant her house was next. She for sure wasn't going to let Swede touch her in any dumb way. She had a feeling that everything would be better if she just started being rid of things. Started from scratch.

She went in Esther's storeroom, where she kept all of Andrea's shirts and other things to restock the shelves. She gathered up the shirts and a box of her pictures.

Andrea strung a boat line between two newly budding willows on the edge of the graveyard. The boat line arched the willow's frail limbs. Andrea hung the T-shirts—black, turquoise, purple, and gold—with Esther's clothespins.

Then came the note cards. She liked to work big, and some of them were magazine-cover size. One was a scene at the creek with two girls on their bellies, their knees bent, heels in the air, and there were dusty-purple salt roses and a heron.

"What are you selling this for?" Swede asked. He had come. He held the card out of the wind.

"Take it," Andrea said.

"No, really."

"For Gawd's sake, I don't want your money. Take it."

Andrea stood with one hand on her hip and waved at the passing cars.

People came out from the store to see the T-shirts. They poked at them as if they were in a department store poking through a rack.

"These for sale?" a man said.

"No, they're free," Andrea said.

"Yes, they're for sale," Swede said.

"Free. Free. Free," Andrea sang.

"Fifteen bucks a shirt," Swede said. "Handcrafted."

"Free to good homes," she said. She went into Esther's and came back with a basket. On it she wrote FREE SHIRTS. She hung the basket on the most weeping branch of the weeping willow.

"Only some are free," Swede explained to a new customer who had been driving by in a patrol car. Andrea thought he was a deputy or something.

"Which ones are free?" the deputy asked Andrea. He didn't see Swede.

108

"It's a come-on," Swede said, trying to stand between them.

"All of them. Everything," Andrea said.

"I don't mind paying," said the deputy. She could tell he was interested in her. He was looking at Andrea, not the shirts.

An older couple shuffled across the parking lot.

Swede said "That one's twenty bucks" to the deputy, who picked up the black one with Andrea's yellow footprints. It had fallen on the ground.

The deputy was confused but he didn't seem to be in a hurry. He sat down on the stone wall. The older couple approached. They had a weimaraner dog. "What's the matter?" Andrea said to the deputy. "No fitting room?"

He grinned and half got up, but Andrea was busy offering things to the couple.

By that time the bus was reloading. People were curious and came over.

"Actually, they're ten dollars," Swede said. He was polite. He walked from customer to customer and said, "Actually, they are ten dollars. They're handcrafted."

"By aborigines," Andrea yelled.

"They're handcrafted by aborigines," Swede told a small child. The child whispered the word back, as if they had a secret. Andrea had hung out fourteen T-shirts. They fluttered, black and white and splashes of color between the willow trees, with the gravestones as background. One by one they got tucked under somebody's arm.

The deputy came up with two shirts draped around his

neck and asked if she lived on the island. He said he'd seen her now and then at Esther's. She was about to answer when Swede came bounding up with his teeth clenched. "That'll be twenty bucks a shirt," he said, almost dancing around the guy.

Esther came out to see about the flea market going on outside her door, and two men in business suits were asking Andrea about some of the scenes. Where had she painted them?

"What if we got married?" Swede said to Andrea.

The men glanced at Swede.

"And go to some post where I could work at McDonald's?" she said.

"You don't have to work at McDonald's."

Esther put her arm around Swede and offered him lunch.

The group more or less disbanded. Nobody wanted to get involved in that situation, not even the deputy.

Andrea had managed to give away every shirt. She and Swede untied the boat line from the wispy willows. The branches curved gracefully, even if they were a little subdued by the weight.

# CHAPTER 12

# The Fifties Dance

SWEDE AND ANDREA DIDN'T HAVE a car, so they walked to Heron Beach after Andrea gave away all her shirts and Swede thought of their getting married. Andrea walked with her lips pressed tight in a straight line, like Sterling's lips. She knew she did.

They walked on the beach and sat in the seaweed. The afternoon sun warmed the sand and she burrowed her feet into it. It got wetter and colder as she dug.

"We don't have to go back to the post," he said, as if they were in the middle of a conversation. "We could take the ferry and get off this place and just work our way along. I had a car," he said. "It's on a jack stand in the auto hobby shop on post. You got me how I'd ever get it back."

She didn't answer, so Swede kept going. "We could buy another junker," he said. "Pretty soon summer places open. We could work easy anywhere up the coast of Maine."

The coast of Maine. She had never been on the coast of Maine. She had only been to Upstate New York and had done that almost gagged and blindfolded for the amount of fun she'd had.

"We don't have to get married," he said. "It's just that everybody on post is married. God, is it lonely. You go to the Enlisted Club and you see these girls in high heels. They stick their heels in the E Club carpet and make circles with their toes. And play Madonna videos and giggle. I could go in there every night of my hitch and never see a girl like you."

Goose bumps ran down her back. She sat with her knees pulled up and her arms wrapped around them and her chin on her knees. She glanced at him. He had taken off his mirrored sunglasses and was looking straight into her eyes. He was sad and reaching out, and she knew there was love there as clearly as she knew the seabirds' names even while they were in flight.

She walked out along the crescent of beach. Then she ran back. She said, "What's it like in Maine?"

"I don't know. You said they had puffins."

Her legs were wet and coated with sand. "You look like a sugar doughnut," he said, and brushed the sand firmly off her legs.

112

□   □   □

The Taggs were on the run. Eleanore, unfortunately, was in charge of supper, which could have been potato cakes, Andrea thought, or it could have been pancakes. But they were truly worth missing. Eleanore was chanting, "Be my, be my baby . . ." She had the spatula and she was queen of the kitchen.

Bess was at the ironing board. Her hair was in pink electric curlers. If it weren't for her perpetually worried brow—and the fact that she was pressing a man's shirt— she could have been a teenager getting ready for a date.

Sterling was on the porch in his undershirt. He brought a Camel to his mouth shielded in his fist. He stood in the open screen door and puffed smoke rings into the light spring air.

"All set, Sterling," Bess called as Andrea went upstairs. She knew Sterling would make Bess stand and hold the checkered shirt outstretched and coax her father off the porch.

Bess wore a slippery, halfway see-through blouse that wasn't like her and made her seem frail. Andrea could see the strap of her slip that dropped over her shoulder. She realized she was imagining her mother and father without her.

"Here," Bess said, "give this to the deserter." She gave her a skinny string tie for Swede to wear.

Swede, Eleanore, and Andrea sat in the backseat of the Valiant like they were all Tagg kids. Swede wore his string tie. He and Sterling braved the trip to the Legion Hall in

113

the dark car in a flowery, heavy haze of Evening in Paris on all the females.

The Legion Hall was pastel green inside. Swede told Andrea it looked a lot like a Quonset hut. Swede danced with the post mistress and Julie the librarian and Bess and numerous Tagg cousins. The band knew three songs. Eleanore and the little kids danced in the back beside the food tables, stuffing heart-shaped cakes and tuna sandwiches in their mouths.

The husbands hung over the bar drinking beer. The women replenished the tables with fancy-cut carrots and clam rolls and slapped the little kids for smearing their cheeks with heart-shaped cakes. The teenagers danced. They slow-danced whenever they wanted to, so it didn't matter that the band knew only three songs.

Andrea cut in on Swede and Bess. "What happened to women's lib?" Swede yelled above the drums. He was talking about all the men at the bar. Then he dipped her.

"Women's what?" she yelled back. "We just got cable." The band was playing an Elvis song.

"Lover boy," Eleanore squealed, burrowing between them. A line of kids followed, playing a version of London Bridge. Swede and Andrea caught them one by one in their arms and turned the dance floor into a carnival of squealing kids.

"Are you always like this?" Andrea asked.

"Like what?"

"I don't know. Courtly."

He turned the dance into a slow dance and wrapped Andrea up in his arms. Polly was dancing with a kid she had always liked. He was a long, skinny, dark-haired boy by whom she measured every boy who asked her out. Tonight she had him. Andrea wished they could slightly bump into her, but Polly looked as if she might break. So might Andrea.

She and Swede had so many things to talk about. But neither of them wanted to talk.

"Keep moving your feet," she said.

"I'm trying," he said.

The band veered off on "Lavender Blue," a sort of new sound for them. Swede held her tightly, and they moved their feet and they both watched the door. "Lavender Blue" was an authentic slow song. Parents and grand-parents got up to dance and they hugged in love knots like the teenagers.

"Come on," Swede said. He and Andrea climbed over the band's instrument cases and slipped out the side door. They sat on the boulder with the names of the lost and missing. The Ladies Auxiliary had put pots of tight yellow marigolds in the tar-kettle planter, and the smell filled the night.

They found Wush sitting on the park bench. "Too loud in there for me," he said.

Swede acted like he'd found a great old friend. He said, "You don't want to sit in the dark."

"I like the dark. I'm twenty years old again, sitting here with time playing tricks. Never mind. If I was asleep, I'd

115

be out on the bay with your grandfather." He squeezed Andrea's hand.

Wush's mind seemed clear. Andrea thought the night did that. The night made him alert and full of memories.

"When the moon was coming back," Wush said, "we had good hauls. In my dreams the moon is always round."

Swede said if they were going to sit in the dark, he'd bring the party out there. He went in and came back with three plates of party food carefully balanced on his arm. They ate tuna-fish sandwiches with the crusts trimmed and celery with pimiento cheese and the little kids' heart cakes.

"Have you ever been to Maine?" asked Andrea.

"Well," he said, "I feel like I went. Winnie had a calendar. It's rocky as the devil up that part of the coast."

Swede and Andrea ate and thought about "rocky as the devil." Swede sat in the middle and all but had his arm around Wush.

"I'll never forget those hot cross buns," he said.

It was then that the car pulled up.

It was a Buick with push-button windows. Andrea would remember that because the driver had trouble finding the buttons to push. They could see her clearly because she had to open her door to talk to them, and she was lit up by the car's interior lights. To her the people on the bench would have been gray shapes. Her hair was in very tight curls all over her head and down her neck, a little like Andrea's image of Cleopatra. She wore a black, gored skirt, a thick silver necklace, and earrings like ingots. Andrea was caught off-guard. She didn't expect the goons to look like this. The woman said she was lost, and Andrea thought, You bet you are.

She called from the car, "Can you tell me where the Legion Hall is?"

It was such a ridiculous question coming from Cleopatra that Andrea looked at Swede before she answered. Swede had a mouth full of celery and was staring at her with pouched cheeks. The woman came a little nearer. Swede swallowed. When the woman was even nearer and Andrea could explore the designs on her earrings, Swede said, "Andrea, this is my mother."

Wush was delighted about having more guests. He wanted to make room for Cleopatra on the bench. But in his excitement he chewed wrong, and his upper dentures slipped. He took them out and snapped them back in. In the meantime Cleopatra was getting her shoes damp in the grass. She looked at her shoes as if she wished somebody would carry her.

"Swede," she said, "they told me at a bar, which is the only place open on this island, that I'd find you here. Where are you staying? I need a long, hot bath. I have been chasing you since yesterday. Why didn't you return my call? Your father knows a colonel who can help."

"This is Andrea Tagg," Swede told her, "and Wush Huckins."

"How do you do," she said.

"Fine" was all Andrea could manage. She felt like the little kid on the beach who sang "Fine, fine."

"Plenty of food," Wush said. He offered her a sandwich.

She was very close then. She glimmered. She didn't look like the kind of person who liked finger tuna sandwiches or people who ate them. And all the Taggs and Swede had just eaten finger tuna sandwiches. And Cleopatra looked like the kind of person who did not like people who had babies when they were fifteen. Cleopatra looked like the kind of person who hired people to have her own babies. She didn't look like she liked dirty people, and Andrea was still dirty from running in the sand. Swede was dirty, too, not to mention absent without leave.

"I'm bushed," Cleopatra said. "Let's go, Swede."

"I'm not going, Mom," he said.

"Where are you staying?"

"I'm camping in the house."

"Is the bathtub in?"

"The house just got walls."

"Then take me to the hotel."

"I don't have a car. You've got a car."

"So how do you get around?"

He glanced at Andrea, and that was a mistake because Cleopatra began taking closer looks at Andrea, now the suspected accomplice, or seductress, or worse. Andrea wished she had combed her hair and not reeked quite so much of Evening in Paris.

Cleopatra said she was going to the Payne House. "I'm very tired," she said. "I need a bath and a shampoo so I can relax."

Andrea looked at her curls and was amazed they were washable. In fact, her own mouth had been open in

118

amazement since the woman had gotten out of the car, and it didn't shut until she drove away.

Swede said, "I just ran out of time."

Andrea would have gone that night. She and Swede went back inside when Cleopatra left. Andrea would have gone then, too, but Swede became very formal and asked for the next dance and all the rest of the dances.

"The last ferry is at midnight," she said.

They talked about working up what Wush had called "rocky-as-the-devil." She would have gone, she told herself. But maybe she thought so because their feet were solid on the Legion Hall floor, and she could catch glimpses of her mother's face. They danced till they were sweaty, fast dances and a jitterbug they made up in which they didn't let go of each other.

By then it was midnight, and they'd have to wait until morning if they were going to go.

# CHAPTER 13

# WAKE

IN THE MORNING IT WAS a little harder. Andrea filled a gym bag to be ready. Swede had finished the roof. He took down his tarp. He'd been there six days and there was a tremendous sense of finality. Something was being wrenched away.

Andrea didn't go to school, but they didn't leave the island, either. They went to Heron Beach to see the nesting terns. They discussed money and a route and what it would take to get a car.

They didn't go. The beach was theirs. The terns glided over them with their feet swinging.

"I wish I saw you . . ." He shaped a circle over his own tough body. "You know, pregnant."

"I was like all those women you see in the grocery store."

"You mean kind of swaybacked and shuffling?"

"Yeah," she said. They laughed. She thought she never laughed so much for feeling so sad.

He put his palm on her belly. It felt solid. They didn't look at each other, but that touch made her feel closer to him than she had felt to anyone before in her life.

A heron alighted on the sand and folded itself into the shape of a heron.

"Your mother came all the way out here," Andrea said. "I think you should go talk to her. Then maybe we can go."

"And you'll talk to your parents now?"

"Yes."

"Then we'll go."

"Yes."

Swede went to see his mother. Andrea helped Bess pack the things they would store until they had another house. Aunt Tessa came—and Aunt May, too. The day turned into a cross between a wake and a covered-dish lunch. Aunt May brought a pot of spaghetti and meatballs. Aunt Tessa brought flounder cookies, and somebody else sent fudge. Andrea would wait until Swede came back. They would eat a lot of spaghetti to hold them. Then she would tell her mother. No, she thought, there was no way to tell her mother. They would just go.

Eleanore ate one of Aunt Tessa's cookies. "I thought so," she said. "They're frozen."

"Well, they keep."

"There's nothing you can chew at Aunt Tessa's," Eleanore said. "She keeps all her food frozen. Once I had a muffin and I was going to save it, but she got it and made it into a brick."

"Shh, Eleanore, she's right there." All the women were in the living room taking down the drapes.

Aunt Tessa had a disease that made her hands shake. When she held a corner of the drape, she used one hand for the drape and the other hand to grab the wrist of the first hand to give it strength.

Andrea watched her hands and waited for Swede to come. Any second he would be at their kitchen table devouring the food. She listened to the women talk.

"Don't just stand around," Aunt Tessa said to Andrea and Eleanore. "I could never just stand around when my mother was working. Get over here and grab on."

"I'm not going to live with her," Eleanore whispered, but the sisters moved shoulder to shoulder toward the working women.

"Come on, come on, hold out your arms," Aunt Tessa commanded. The girls held out their arms to receive folds of dusty drapes. Andrea wished she had taken the keys to the Valiant. Swede would be there and back by now.

Aunt Tessa stumbled a little. She also had a bum knee, which Andrea suspected was not a football injury. Aunt Tessa's sport was rummy, which she did not play with children. Popper had raised three kids on his own in that house after Andrea's grandmother died. Sterling said he remembered Aunt Tessa's rowing up the creek to give Popper a hand. Andrea had asked her father if Aunt Tessa was nicer then, if they ever had fun. "Hell, no," he said. "We were double work to her. She had her own kitchen to scrub. No fun about it."

They brought down folds upon folds of drapery until the living room was undressed and embarrassedly white. While they were undressing it, the women talked about beetles on the raspberries. Bess said if she picked off one, she picked off one hundred and one last summer. Aunt May said Popper needed new facecloths up to the home. His were getting ratty. They had almost buried Eleanore in insulation-backed brocade.

They all knew what they were doing; they were packing up the last of the Taggs. It was a little like the second hand come to grab hold of Bess and keep her strong. They didn't have to talk about the obvious.

Aunt Tessa was a nasty, mean woman. She never showed mercy in her manner. She had a hide as tough as the ornate shell of a sea turtle. That reminded Andrea of the mysteries revealed on the seaman Queequeg's tattooed skin. The woman's kindness today confused Andrea so much, she grabbed Aunt Tessa by the arms and kissed her tough cheek. Then she ran out the door because Swede should be coming down the road.

Sterling pulled in the driveway. That meant it was already lunchtime. She listened to his truck door crunch closed. Swede had not come. "No school?" Sterling said.

"I didn't go," Andrea said.

"Who's here?"

"Everybody," she said. "They all brought food."

Sterling hesitated on the doorsill. "Tide's out," he said. He looked at her. His eyes were no less piercing. "Let's go dig some clams," he said.

Andrea's stomach felt like one hard knot. Sterling took off his cap and put it back on, on the back of his head. They hadn't clammed together, they hadn't set foot in the skiff together, since last year. "Or you don't do that no more," he said, turning away. "On account of it's flesh."

"I think they're waiting on you for lunch," she said.

Eleanore brought bread and peanut butter and jelly down to the dock where Andrea sat. She spread the bread and handed Andrea a thick, gooey sandwich. When the new leaflets on the willow moved in the wind and cast flickering shadows on the dock, Andrea thought that would be him. She heard all the sounds from the road.

"Who will live here?" Eleanore said. "I wonder if they'll have kids." She was just wondering out loud, and Andrea looked up at the porch and wondered who would sit there and smear suntan lotion on each other's shoulders. And wear Noxzema on their noses.

That's when Swede came around the corner. He didn't make any noise, and Andrea would never have heard him, anyway. Eleanore made him a thick, gooey sandwich. Swede knelt down. "We have to wait," he said. Swede didn't eat. He tossed the sandwich from hand to hand, and she felt his eyes on her always.

She looked at him. "It doesn't matter," she said.

"No," he said, "we just have to wait."

They went indoors, and Swede spent the afternoon letting himself be bossed around by the aunts.

They sent Sterling back to work, but they kept Swede. Sterling stopped and lectured on the right way to refinish the bureau, which he had talked about doing all Andrea's life. And on the best way to polish an unearthed silver fruit compote he had never polished. "For Gawd's sake, go back to the boat yard," Aunt Tessa said.

Swede worked like a water buffalo. He hauled anything. Once, when he passed Andrea, he said, "Goddamn her, I'd almost re-up just to see her face."

"Who?"

"Wendy."

He called Cleopatra, Wendy.

# CHAPTER 14

# PAYNE HOUSE

WHEN THE AUNTS WERE GONE and it was near supper-time, Andrea and Swede found Eleanore in the kitchen with one of Bess's aprons tied around her chest. She was a machine that made a variety of noises—*slam, shatter, smash, bang, thud, clatter, tingle*.

"I'm cooking," she said.

"What are you cooking?" Swede said.

"Noodles."

"And what?"

"That's all we have. Noodles." And sure enough, a pot began to ooze, bubbling water like a volcano onto the stove and the floor. "Mom's going to be mad," Eleanore said. She sounded weary. Andrea lifted the lid of the pot and turned down the temperature.

Bess came in. She was wearing the new skirt she got for the Fifties Dance, only without the petticoat. When she sat down, it doubled up at the waist. She had girlish curls. Swede, Eleanore, and Andrea sat with her at the kitchen table.

"How would you like to go out to dinner?" she asked.

No one answered. The family didn't go out much. "Eleanore made noodles," Andrea said.

Eleanore said, "That's okay."

"It's a treat," Bess said.

"Where would we go?" Eleanore said.

"Payne House."

Eleanore nodded. "Do we have to wash the windows?"

"No, it's a treat. Mrs. Stuhr invited us."

"Mrs. Stuhr?" Andrea said. "You know her?"

"This morning she was here to see her house," Bess said. Swede went to watch the noodles ooze over.

"Did she invite Dad, too?" Andrea said.

"Don't be ridiculous. Of course she did."

Andrea waited for Swede to explain.

"She invited all of us," Bess said. "Half past six to the Payne House. She said seven, but I know Sterling couldn't hold out that long for supper."

Bess herded Swede and the Taggs up the wrought-iron staircase to Payne House at half past six. A woman with a turquoise necklace and black hair pulled tight to the nape

127

of her neck stood at a podium. By the light of a small brass lamp she checked off their reservation. Swede and Andrea stood together. Bess wouldn't let Andrea wear jeans and a mow-your-own-grass shirt. Andrea had said she'd wear a turtleneck underneath to dress it up, but Bess said no. Now Andrea wore a short paisley skirt with a slit on the side and a matching jacket in a fabric that looked a lot like a couch cover. She had paint still under her fingernails and on her feet.

Wendy Stuhr came down from her room very near seven, after all. She smiled and took Sterling's big, grizzled hand for a longer time than Andrea thought she had to. She wore a tight, slim dress that came to her ankles and her hair in the same jet spirals. Andrea sat down in a white wicker chair and crossed her almost naked legs. Swede sat next to her so close that Wendy looked at Andrea with her dark, exotic eyes. She sat across from Andrea. Andrea thought, Here is the woman who *owns* the World of Beauty. Andrea couldn't take her eyes off her. She began at the delicate azure circles Wendy drew around her eyes and worked down her body to the textured diamonds across her swaying foot. She looked at her mother, who had sat down and was making small talk about island things.

At that moment Andrea would have done anything to make her mother at ease, to make her brag about the is-land schools and the way the town did snow removal and creek dredging. If they were home, Aunt Tessa would have brought half of an angel food cake out of her freezer. She would have opened out the white freezer paper and left it to soften, but it wouldn't have, quite. And they would have sawed-off wedges to pass around. Wendy would probably have only held hers stiffly and smiled that smile she was smiling now.

Bess wondered out loud what kind of pastries they'd made with her eggs. A picture of the clipper ship, *The Flying Cloud,* was on the parlor wall. Sterling told Wendy about the relation he had who had been first mate on *The Flying Cloud.* Wendy didn't answer, so Sterling went on to tell the entire history of the clipper ship. He said it was the end of whaling. Everybody wanted to sail on a clipper ship.

Wendy smiled and signaled to the hostess that their pleasantries were over and they'd like to be seated.

She reeled off the names of French wines to the waiter and ordered something with grenadine for the children. That was Eleanore and Andrea. She winked at them as if they were adorable.

"I'm not hungry," Andrea whispered to Swede, who never looked at his mother. "What's this about? Is she paying us back for not calling the cops on you?"

"Eat it, anyway," he whispered. "This may be the last meal we get for a while."

"There's Aunt May's spaghetti," Andrea said. "We could pack that."

The waiter brought drinks. Very cautiously, Eleanore poured her grenadine in the flower vase and turned the rose's water pink. Andrea looked at the bubbles by candlelight. The room was dark. The walls were covered in purple velvetlike wallpaper and paintings of crumbling English manor houses.

They ordered French things in terrible accents. Eleanore buttered pumpernickel rolls for Sterling. And Wendy told her opinion of the Army. "All volunteer Army," she said. "Swede's father is crazy. He was a West Point man," Wendy explained. "There was no reasoning with him."

Their dinners were served on deep blue plates trimmed in gold. Sterling said his wasn't enough to feed a rabbit. "It's French," Bess explained. "Very rich."

"I know it's French," he growled.

There was asparagus mousse with green things and dollops of vegetables arranged in crescents. It looked a little like a children's party. Sterling poured salt in his hand to sprinkle on his dollop of meat and tossed the extra over his shoulder, oblivious to Wendy's gaze. Maybe she would tell it back West as an island custom.

After dinner the waiter asked if they wanted dessert.

"Of course," Bess said.

"Bring on the desserts," said Sterling.

The pastry chef knew Bess and brought the trolley personally. He wheeled it inches from Bess's curious eyes. The waiter pointed out his strawberry crepes. "Two eggs, Mrs. Tagg." His creme patissières. "Five egg yolks, Mrs. Tagg." Chocolate soufflé. "Six, Mrs. Tagg." The waiter was truly pleased to have her. He said, "Your table shall have a platter. You shall taste them all."

Wendy was getting restless. She was not interested in pastries. While they were all chewing, she said, "I'm delighted we've reached an understanding."

130

"About what?" Andrea said.

Bess said, "Not everybody in the family heard."

"Heard what?" said Eleanore.

Bess's gaze passed over Andrea. It made her suspect she was not going to like what she was about to hear.

"I'll tell it," Sterling said.

"I don't have any problem with that," Wendy said. She toyed with her black spirals.

Sterling was to the point. He said, "She bought our house."

"Who?" Andrea said. She couldn't believe.

"Her." He pointed at Wendy.

Andrea looked at Swede. "No," she said. "You wouldn't buy our house."

Andrea studied her father's closed face to find something more than that. "You sold our house to Swede?"

Sterling shrugged. "They're paying a hell of a lot of money." His voice was low.

Andrea shut her eyes. Her head whirled like she was on a ride with Polly, and she opened them for relief. She didn't get any.

"It's not as if we're in the street," Sterling said.

"I knew it had been on the market for some time," Wendy said. "It's an adorable cottage, Mr. Tagg."

"It's no cottage," Sterling said. "My grandmother raised five sons and daughters in it, and my father raised three of us after my mother died. They brought her bed in the front room. She wanted to hear the seabirds while she was dying. I remember that big wood bed square in the middle of the front room when I was a kid."

131

Bess sat with her hands in her lap. She had emptied her glass. A waiter came and filled it.

"Don't waste your food," Bess said to Andrea and Eleanore. She picked up her fork and diligently ate her own cream puff.

Andrea was stunned. She didn't want to look at Swede's face. She didn't want to know him, and she didn't want to see him. And at the very same time, he was everything she was looking forward to. He was how she was getting through. She walked out of the dining room, barely aware of her father's insistent command to "sit down, sit down if you know what's good for you." His voice was a shadowy background.

She went back to the parlor and sat in one of the heavy upholstered wing chairs for queens.

"Your house was for sale. Somebody was going to buy it," Swede said. He had followed her.

"Like hell."

"You knew it was for sale."

Andrea peeled paint out from under her nails. She went in the door marked MESDAMES, where he couldn't come. She washed her hands with soap shaped like scallop shells. The Mesdames had a chaise lounge with gold arms. She sat on the chaise lounge to dry her hands with monogrammed hand towels. They had been warmed. Of all the things to think about, she thought of her baby. They had given her a warm blanket. A huge, warmed white blanket to wrap herself warm in after the baby came. She sat back in the chaise lounge and dropped the towel over her head.

In her couch-cover suit she thought maybe she blended into the upholstery.

No way. "I didn't buy it," Swede said. Andrea took off the towel. Swede had come in with an elderly woman in a Florida-bright pantsuit. She dabbed rouge on her cheeks, and in the mirror her eyes flitted from boy to girl to boy.

"I didn't buy it," he repeated. "I've got about four bucks on me, and I'm on the run."

The lady's eyes popped. Her right cheek was very rosy.

"Look," Andrea said, "I don't want to talk to you. I don't care what you do. It's not your fault you own my house."

"I don't. My mother does. She owns a lot of houses." He was trying to grab her hand and she could smell his after-shave. He hadn't worn after-shave before. The smell of it made it seem like them against us.

"Then she rents it back if the people promise to be good tenants?" Andrea got up. She had to get away from him. The smell of the after-shave was making her sick to her stomach.

"You aren't even honest," she said.

"I didn't do it."

"You make me sick."

"Nobody did it. Your house was for sale."

She said, "The boys on the beach insult you, but then they split. At least they split. Goddamn, you go to hell. You got it all. And it won't be your fault when she turns every other room into a bathroom like Tocci's."

133

"She bought it for the land. She wanted the land." He turned away after he spilled out the worst.

"Or when they bring the wrecking crews for the henhouse. And my house. I don't care what you do," she said again, and left him there to stink up Mesdames with the rosy lady.

She knew the signs of contractors with clever names checkered the island. Pretty soon there would be a sign for JACKBUILT, INC., where she and Bess should have been selling suncatchers.

# CHAPTER 15

# First Place

SHE RAN. AND THE HARDER she ran, the madder she was. She ran down the wrought-iron Payne House stairs. She might have run all the way to the creek, but she saw a kid she knew from school. She stood in the middle of the road and waved her arm through the beam of his headlights.

It was Danny Loiselle. When he stopped, she shoved in beside him. He smelled of English Leather, but she was used to that on him. She wedged herself next to him because he was hot, and Danny couldn't take anything away from her.

"Take me home, would you, Danny?"

He was warm and he only stank a little.

"How about I take you over to Baytown, to Spite Malice's, baby?"

"No, just home," she said.

"Or Acapulco."

"Thanks," she said. "Just the creek." And he got her there, and she didn't have to explain why she was shaking all the way.

She walked down the road from her house to Swede's. She had on shoes that tapped on the tar. There was a new moon. She couldn't see her own hand.

She went in what would be the front door. Then she climbed the stairs. They weren't the real stairs. They were Uncle Clint's work stairs. From the top she couldn't see much. She felt like an animal with poor vision who depended on other senses because she could feel the barn-size, cavernous space that she watched grow. She went as high up in the rafters of the cathedral ceiling as she could climb.

She knew the cross beams reached high into the roof. It was a crazy show of angles and geometry that made her think of her extra-credit star. She used to come, before Swede, and watch the fish hawks, and before they came back in March, she watched the sparrows. Now it was dead quiet. Even the sparrows were asleep. She climbed up to a temporary attic floor Uncle Clint had made with a few pieces of plywood across the beams.

"Whoever walks in that door, I will kill you!" she said

136

quietly. Of course, nobody came. She screamed to hear how it sounded, and the scream bounced all around her. This was her house before it was anybody's. She watched it. She sat in its rafters. She liked the smell of its wood. It was more her house than Cleopatra's.

Nobody came for her to kill or even scream at. She thought of things she could do. She could go get somebody and bring them back here and kill them. She could jump. She could burn this monster down. It was too big for Tagg Creek.

Nobody came. All her ideas appealed to her. They were about herself. It was she who would jump, it was she who would burn, it was she who would die.

She sat down on the plywood, and when she did, she felt something hard in her pocket. It was the wooden plaque strung on green yarn that she dropped there. FIRST PLACE: BEAUTY PAGEANT. Right, she thought, big deal at a dinky island firemen's fair. She ran her finger over the letters burned into the wood. Those firemen were blind. Maybe blind drunk on beer, and Springsteen pounding in a hot July breeze when she and Polly and all the others half strutted, half huddled in hysterics around the Ferris wheel for the competition. Anyway, the firemen were dead wrong.

The world is screwed up, she told the monster house. And I am ugly. She hung the wooden heart around her neck. Nobody came.

Andrea sat in the rafters waiting for somebody to come in so she could kill them. She sat wide-awake, waiting for

137

somebody to come to take the blame for how bad she hurt
and take the sick, tight knot out of her stomach. At midnight, still nobody had come. Not even to drag her out
and tell her she was as stupid as a loon and was done even
before she got started. It was cold and she began to shiver.

I hate you, Swede Stuhr. She told him three times.
Short marriage, she thought. Now that she was free of
him, she didn't have to like anybody in the entire world.

She went on thinking thoughts like those for a long
time. She went on doing it until about three in the morning, when she must have woken up a chickadee. He set to
whistling a full ten minutes without a break. Andrea sat in
her skirt like slipcovers and realized around three o'clock
that probably nobody would come.

The idea grabbed her hard by the heels and the head and
kind of wrenched her. Bess was packing, fussing over
cameo pins and cherry pitters and cotton floss. What was
her mother going to do without a house? Sterling was lost
in a world of taxes and closing costs. Swede was in a hotel
with a bed and hot water to shave and people to dry-clean
his BDUs and shine his boots. It was three o'clock on an
April morning with a chickadee on a marathon whistle
binge, and Andrea in the rafters with her knees wedged
tight to her belly in her slipcover party clothes.

It wasn't all bad, the idea that nobody was coming. It
took some of the knot out of her stomach. She realized her
teeth had been clenched because she stopped clenching
them. The chickadee was whistling again. Andrea had herself. A huge relief came with that idea. She felt free to

know she was on her own and she had herself. She felt a touch of power, and it wasn't just the height of her perch. She felt free.

By four o'clock the gulls woke up. She listened to their screech, and the sparrows started fluttering in the roof.

Someone came through the doorway. There was some light then, and Andrea could see Eleanore. Eleanore found Andrea right away, being gaudy and singular up in the rafters. Eleanore began to climb as if Andrea were in a normal place.

"Are you going to sleep here tonight?" Eleanore asked.

"Maybe," said Andrea.

"At least then I'll know."

"What?"

"Not to wait up."

"You waited up all night?"

"Yes."

Eleanore had the brains to wear her winter coat. She climbed carefully, and when she got to Andrea, she made a little bed with her coat in the space between the attic rooms. She dropped half her coat on Andrea's shivering body. Eleanore was wearing her bumpy cotton pajamas. She bundled under the other half of the coat. There in the rafters with the morning songs growing to a mighty pitch, Eleanore went to sleep. Andrea sat very still, feeling puffs from her sister's breath on her hand.

Andrea's eyes were well adjusted to the dim light and she recognized Swede as the next person who stood in the door. His blond head was a beacon.

He spotted her in the rafters. "It's cold out there," he said.

"I know," she said. Their voices bounced off the walls.

"I mean in the hammock. Well," he said, "at least it's not raining."

"You slept in the hammock?" She watched him come. He had a small box under his arm the size of a take-out meal box.

"You could say I laid in it for a lot of hours. It's never been super comfortable."

"I thought you were at the hotel in a bed."

"Are you going to throw something at me when I get close enough?" he said about halfway up.

She thought of the FIRST PLACE: BEAUTY PAGEANT plaque in her pocket. She could throw that. She didn't answer.

Eleanore rolled over and began to snore.

"Good," he said.

He was up to their level. His after-shave had worn off, but nothing else had. Andrea's heart pounded. She had not counted on this. She squeezed her eyes shut tight and felt the vibration his footsteps made as he walked across the boards. Damn, she thought. Oh, shit, I like him anyway. Holding on to yourself didn't stop that.

"Are you going to kick me when I get close enough?"

"Yes," she said.

"I love you," he said when he got to her. He saw Eleanore and began to whisper. "I've been trying to quit," he said. He was apologizing.

140

"That's okay," she said.

Swede stretched out on her other side. She heard the fish hawk family around. Eleanore snored. Swede put his head on her thigh but that was too bony, so he moved up and she gave him a corner of Eleanore's coat. The box was between his feet.

"There's an apartment complex outside the gate at the post where a lot of married guys live," Swede said. "I wouldn't call it nice, but the wives like it all right. Some of them have kids. The guys have to get up in the night. They're always talking about stunts their babies pull."

"What's that?" she said. Swede's Happy Meal was rustling.

"A bribe," he said. He reached down for the box and gave it to her. It flipped open as if it were a take-out meal, but inside something peeped. She reached in and pulled out a baby chick.

He said, "You can't see, but it's blue."

It was soft. Its heart beat against her hand. "Where'd you get a blue chick?"

"Baytown."

"You went to Baytown?"

"I was going to catch a bus."

"Instead you bought a chick."

"I wish it was a rooster," he said.

"It will be if it lives. They don't like to be dyed."

"How do you know it's male?"

"The cockerels get culled from the brood. They're the

141

ones sold for Easter chicks." She put the chick back in the box so he wouldn't fall off the attic boards.

"Come with me," he said.

She didn't know what to say. He had her hand. She felt his jaw against her stomach. He had a wide, square jaw.

This was a Wednesday morning. A regular school day. If she went to school, people would still be talking about the Fifties Dance and who was with who. It was a world away. She vaguely remembered geometry homework. She wondered if she could draw a picture of the cross beams in Swede Stuhr's roof.

She knew of three ways to raze a house. She wondered how Swede's mother would hire it done. She could take it down carefully, board by board. Or she could bulldoze it in about twenty minutes. Or she could lease it to the firemen, and they could torch it and use it as a firemen's experiment.

When she came back, if she went with Swede, there wouldn't be any sign of them—her family.

But she imagined herself in Swede's apartment.

"What do you want?" he said.

"You mean like if I could have anything?"

"Yeah."

"Dumb things," she said.

"What's one?"

"I want to cook you something dumb like angel food cake from scratch and watch you eat it all. And you'd think I was really something because I could make angel food like my mother's." She kissed his fingers the way he'd kissed hers that day in the library. Yesterday.

"Your father really wanted to sell," Swede said.

"You already said that."

The chick was getting carried away peeping, having found there was life outside the box. Eleanore was on her back, snoring. It was light enough to see the beginning of dawn through the rough windows.

"So, anyway, I think we should both go," he said.

At five-thirty Swede carried Eleanore down the rough stairs. He put her in his sleeping bag and made sure she was wrapped in her coat and his poncho. It was a very cold spring. Andrea wrote a note on the chick's box. She wrote, "Dear Eleanore, this is for us from Swede. Would you feed him, please? I'll do the dishes for you someday. Love, A." Eleanore didn't wake up.

Andrea got her gym bag. Swede had his pack. They borrowed the Valiant and caught the first ferry.

# CHAPTER 16

# BABIES

THEY PARKED A SHORT WAY from Spite Malice on Main Street and walked down the cement walk among people. They walked with an old lady in pink, a little pink wrap-around that came to her knees and a pink hat. She walked as if she had no place in particular to go. Across the street, a man paused at the bookshop's window display. He wore a camera mounted with a telephoto lens and looked at the lady in pink and a lone fisherman in the distance with professional curiosity. Some kids taunted one another at the corner. Real life set in.

When Andrea and Swede had walked to his house to hammer, they knew where they were going and what they

were going to do if it was only for the next twenty minutes. But walking down Main Street in Baytown, even
with their bags over their shoulders, they weren't sure. Andrea remembered what Swede had said after Wendy left
the Legion Hall dance. He said, "I just ran out of time."
That feeling of finality crept back in, and it didn't feel like
they could stall it anymore.

They stopped at a diner. Swede had a little money. He
had enough for ferry passage to New London and bus
fare. He counted it on the table.

Andrea had her milky coffee and Swede had a Coke.
Swede wouldn't talk. He was doing a lot of rubbing of his
sprouting head. Then he rubbed his jaw.

"So don't go back," Andrea said.

Swede knocked over his glass by accident. They watched
the Coke make a puddle around a dirty ashtray. "Shit," he
said. He turned and faced the window. He cracked his
knuckles, one deafening joint after the other.

"Look, Swede," she said. "We could go back to the island for a while."

"I can't."

"Why not?"

"You know why not."

"All right, I know why not."

"If I went back," he said, "I know I'd go for Wendy's
throat."

Andrea thought that had a nice ring to it.

He glanced at her, and they both knew they were running out of time.

"Come on," she said. She took his hand.

"Where?"

"I don't know, but we have to get out of here."

They left the diner. She wanted to walk, so they left the Valiant parked in the street. They walked with even their hips touching. Once Andrea saw two people who weren't kids anymore walking along, and they each had a hand tucked in the other's back pockets. Their jeans were tight, so their hands were wedged in there. They did not want to lose each other. At the time Andrea thought they looked silly, but she understood it now.

Swede was wearing his mirrored sunglasses again. When he talked to Andrea, he pushed them up on his head. But walking down the street, he wore them for the world.

They walked past Popper's nursing home. Andrea stopped in front of a sharply inclined, double-wide driveway thickly planted with arborvitae and other remorselessly green and sprawling things. It was the city hospital, and she looked up the drive to the stone stairs and the revolving door she knew was at the top.

"What if we walked up there?" she said.

"I'd rather get thrown in the stockade," he said.

She kept looking up through the arborvitae, and Swede said, "I'd rather go on starvation rations. I like nurses about as much as you."

She nodded and started walking up the driveway with him.

"Are we sick?"

"Pretty sick," she answered.

146

BABIES

They pushed through the revolving door.

A woman in a booth told them visiting hours started after eight o'clock. It was only seven-fifteen.

"Who are we visiting?" he asked.

"I'm not sure," Andrea said.

"A generic visit," Swede said to the lady in the booth.

"I'm sorry," the lady said. "You have to be related."

"We are," Andrea said.

"Who's the patient?" The lady in the information booth stood up to hear better.

"We're visiting my aunt."

"And the name?"

Andrea picked a common island name, and sure enough, there was a patient there to match it. The lady seemed to have discharged enough of her duty and sank inside her booth.

Swede sat down and held his nose. He said the smell of hospitals made him sick. Andrea paced. "We might not stay," she said. "It's just an idea."

She rebraided her hair, looking into the mirrors over Swede's eyes. She worked her hair into a smooth, thick French braid. Sometimes Swede anchored a section because now and then her fingers gave way and she had no strength at all. She put on lipstick and smoothed her suit. She realized she hadn't taken time to change.

Bess wore a dark suit when she took Andrea to the home. That day was like a funeral. Now Andrea wore a gaudy, paisley, side-slit party suit. Andrea studied the hos-

147

pital floor plan. At eight o'clock she grabbed Swede's hand and they shot through the swinging doors.

She led Swede to the third floor, D wing, where they emerged from an elevator, took the first right, and stopped face-to-face with a row, behind glass, of yawning, stretching, wrinkle-lipped, mottled, and dozing babies. Swede said, "Holy shit."

They were ugly things, for sure. Andrea stood transfixed and studied them one after the other. After a long time she looked around for Swede and found him propped against the corridor wall. She said, "Do you think my little girl was this ugly?"

Swede eyed the babies. "My guess is she'd fit right in," he said.

Andrea smiled. All the babies were in glass boats, and Andrea imagined her daughter in one. Other families were in the hall, too, looking at the babies in the boats. They laughed.

"There she is," they said. "The one with the triple chin."

"I'm going to tell her you said that."

That one's name was Pauline Jayne. It said so on her boat.

"What do you want to bet," Swede whispered, "she got Pauline from the grandmother." He nodded at a grinning fool of a lady with tears dripping from her eyes.

Baby Pauline was exhausted. She slept as though she had a good three nights to make up for. A woman in a gown and mask waved at the family on the other side. She didn't just wave. She waved and grinned and lifted her

148

mask and mouthed words so that the family all made guesses about what she was trying to say. Andrea soon gathered this was the baby's mom.

When the mom picked up tiny Pauline, Pauline drooped in exhaustion on her shoulder. Her little spine curved so that if her mom had not cupped Pauline's shoulder in her palm—even if she did it like Pauline was made of tissue paper—Pauline would have curved right around like a caterpillar. She heaved her arm over her mom's arm and let her face sag on her mom's shoulder. She sighed.

The family sighed in unison.

"She's our first," explained the grandmother to Swede and Andrea. "Who did you come to see? Is one yours?"

Andrea shook her head because she didn't trust herself to talk. She gripped Swede's hand tightly.

"Not any one in particular," Swede said. "We just came to see."

The grandmother looked at them knowingly and grinned and cried. "Look at ours, then!" she exclaimed. "By all means."

The mom came out of the nursery. Andrea wanted to ask her question after question. The nurses began wheeling the babies in a parade out the door of the nursery, all the babies in their boats.

"Come on with us." It was the mom. She was talking to Andrea. "Come see ours. It's feeding time."

Andrea could see the grandmother put her up to it.

"You, too," the mom said to Swede.

He looked behind himself, playing as though she had to

be talking to somebody else. "No, you," she said. They laughed. Andrea and Swede got caught up in the joy of Pauline's family. They were boisterous, telling each other "Shhh, heavens to Betsy! Will you shhh" all the way to the room.

The mom sat down and the nurse put Pauline in her lap. Her family sounded like they were at a baseball game, but they didn't wake up Pauline. Then the dad held her. Then the grandma. Then the grandpa. The grandma seemed very touched by Swede and Andrea. Who knows what she made of them, Andrea thought. But she took the green mask off the grandfather and gave it to Andrea. She pulled over a chair.

Andrea sat, and the mom put Pauline, just for a second, in the crook of Andrea's arm. Andrea felt the weight of her tiny head. Pauline wore a white T-shirt and one bootie. She must have left one in her boat. Her bare foot was pink as a sea star. Andrea watched her tiny lips and tiny nose and fingernails, with tiny moons that made her seem as though she were a person. Andrea tasted salt and realized she was crying, but there wasn't anything she could do about that. So she cried and thought babies did not need yellow kimonos; they looked good in white T-shirts.

And then it was over. The mom picked her up. She glanced at Swede and raised her eyes as if to say, "What next?" But she let Swede hold her baby so he'd know, too. Swede gave Andrea his sunglasses, and he held Pauline in his burly arms.

Pauline spread her tiny fingers in the air. That was when

BABIES

everyone realized she was coming to. Swede gave her back
to her mom just before she exploded in wails and fit right
into her family with baseball-game lungs.

Swede and Andrea left.

They walked a long time without saying much. There
was the smallest pressure on Andrea's forearm from the
weight of the baby's head. Andrea thought she must still
be crying, but she didn't mind, and neither did Swede.

She hoisted the gym bag on her shoulder. Her sandals
flapped on the sidewalk.

"I don't feel so bad," she said.

"Good," he said. "When do you think you'll stop crying?"

"I'm not sure," she said.

They came to the Valiant where they had parked it on
Main Street by the deli. They got in, and Swede climbed
over the gears so that they sat in the same bucket seat.
They held on to each other, and she buried her face in his
neck. She thought maybe they were both thinking of the
married apartments outside the gate to his post with the
people up all night walking babies. There would be swing
sets and see-saws, all that stuff.

"I'm turning myself in," he said. "Before my mother ar-
ranges something."

"What'll they do to you?"

"What can they do? They already killed me off. The rest
is gravy."

"What's the gravy part?"

151

"I don't know. But whatever it is, we could make it. They can't hang me."

Andrea straightened up and blew her nose. For the first time she put herself in Swede's place. She realized how lonely he was. He hated what he did. He owed more time. And he was related to Wendy with the possibility of having to see her again in his future. Andrea thought she, herself, could manage to miss Wendy forever, even if circumstance sat them at the same table again.

Andrea almost told Swede she loved him, too, but she couldn't say that. All she could do was blow her nose. At least she could touch him. And she had held a baby. She had held Aunt Tessa by the shoulders. At that moment she liked herself, too.

"I might get through school," she said.

Swede nodded.

"I never thought I would before. You taught me how to skip four hundred pages."

"That's not why," he said.

"I know."

She looked at him. "I guess I love you, though," she said.

"Great," he said. "I'll have that on my tombstone. 'She guessed she loved me, though.'"

"No, say she did."

"She did. Are we still engaged?"

"I don't think so," she said. "We just met. How come I love you this bad?"

Swede almost cracked a joke. She could see it coming,

but then he shook his head and he held on to her and she held on to him. It was so good, even as she realized they possibly would not marry, they possibly would not see each other again, and possibly if they did, it would never be this good. So they held on like scalers of mountains.

"Okay," he finally said. "So what's your address?" Andrea took a pen from the glove compartment and wrote it on his hand. "Andrea Tagg, Tagg Creek, Manhanset Island, Long Island, New York."

"We don't have house-to-house," she managed to say. "I'll get it at the post office."

He said it sounded like an address for the goddamn birds.

Andrea drove Swede back down to Orient Point. He got a ticket on the ferry just heading out, so there wasn't a lot of waiting, and no time for many words or any kissing. He scribbled his address on her palm because it was all they could find. "This is it until I know different," he said, and climbed the passenger ramp.

She saw him on the upper deck, up on top of the coiled ropes, waving like a lunatic.

The horn blasted and she waved like a lunatic back.

When she returned to the island, it was still only nine-thirty in the morning. She didn't feel like facing whatever she would have to face at home, so she went on to school. It was second period. Almost time for art, but not quite. It was still English. She opened the door to Markworthy's class and went to her desk. Markworthy had his hands raised in a dramatic moment. He was talking about the Age of Realism, and as he talked, he dug through the papers in his briefcase. When he found what he was looking for, he glanced at Andrea. He came and dropped the paper on her desk. It was the essay exam. One thing she could say for Markworthy was that he was fast. Two days max. She had written seven pages. At the end was an 82. In Markworthy's typically anal style he had printed, in minuscule red letters that for anybody but his students would require a magnifying glass, "Good."

# CHAPTER 17

# Low
# Tide

It was Saturday morning and the tide was out. Andrea knew because she slept on the porch, and she could tell by the quiet. Everything seemed quieter at low tide. The sea animals hid.

Swede would be back at the post. She told herself it was too soon to start looking for mail.

They would move out in two weeks. Only they might as well have already moved out, Andrea thought, because Bess had cleaned everything and the family wasn't allowed to use it. She didn't allow anybody even to bake a potato in the oven. No one had told Bess the property had been sold for the land. Andrea wasn't going to tell her. Sterling wasn't going to tell her. So nobody used the oven, and they all faithfully scrubbed the tub. The house had never looked so good. Sterling even fixed the porch step.

When Sterling got up, he asked Andrea again if she'd be up to going clamming. Her mouth was dry, and she had been listening to the quiet a long time. She went in the bathroom and pulled on her jeans and her shirt. She grabbed Sterling's jacket off the back of the door. He didn't yell at her, nothing about "You'd think you didn't have any clothes of your own." Andrea thought they all hurt too bad to fight. She just wore the jacket. She got a drink of water from the tap.

The skiff was tied up at one of the dock pilings. The dock was missing every other plank, and the planks that remained weren't all that steady. Sterling took the tiller.

He hunched over his old one-lung engine and hauled back on the cord. It sputtered and caught. He kept the motor at a slow hum and seemed to move the boat more by his will, the way he still stood, leaning over the tired engine. He was heading for the point. She straddled the clam rakes and faced the wind head-on. Sterling was in no rush. It was barely dawn. It reminded Andrea of the morning when the girl in *A White Heron* climbed a tree to see the heron and the ocean.

They slowly moved to the mouth of the still-asleep creek. They eased past people's docks and picture windows and Wush's porch screen. The next cottage was surrounded by a fortress of daffodils. A person couldn't have walked up the bank to the door without downing a dozen, the yard was so thick with them. A night heron screamed and flew over with its orange legs stretched out behind.

"It's a terrific low tide," Sterling said.

That was good, Andrea knew, when the water washed back and exposed more stretches of sand.

Sterling eased around the point of land where Tocci's place stood. Tocci's was made of rectangles and circles of cedar and glass that stretched up and out over the bay. Once Andrea tied up at Tocci's dock when he wasn't there, which he usually wasn't. She pretended she lived there and waved to the people on Windsurfers. The front of the house was nearly all glass. Tocci's lights had paper-lantern shades. It looked like he brought the moon inside. Paper-lantern moons shone from his glass house.

Sterling brought the boat around Tocci's dock, where it jutted out at a right angle into the bay.

It wasn't like Sterling to bother about this beach. They'd never dug a clam here all her life. "Grab a rake," he said. Sterling jumped out, and when Andrea was on the beach, he drew the boat up. A few days ago she would have panicked at the idea of facing Tocci. Now she was with her father and she suspected her father knew something about the gash of silver on the Valiant and maybe the gash of red on the Volvo.

"Go on," he said. "Good here as anywhere." They walked across the muddy sand watching for bubbles spouting up through the sand. She dug in her rake gently because these were the soft shells they were after. She dropped her catch in the bucket. Sterling took slow and careful steps, watching for the clams' spray. They kept on digging, moving back and forth across the flats off Tocci's beach until the lights clicked on. It was a loud click. Tocci had torchlights.

"Get away from my dock," they heard him call.

"Public waters," Sterling called back.

Andrea watched him, lit up by the light. His hair was turning silver and it glistened in Tocci's light. He had a rim of the moon behind him and the cries of birds as a frame. His gaze was cool and gray and never flinched. He put on a good show. She had to give him credit.

"Keep on," Sterling said. The light was good now to watch for the shoots of water from the piss clams. Andrea kept on digging.

"Get off my beach or I call the police," Tocci said.

"We got rights to the high-water mark," Sterling said. Tocci would know that was the law. Any islander had fishing rights in island waters up to the high-water mark, even if Tocci and others didn't like it.

"You've got no right at my dock," Tocci called back. He didn't call Sterling "Tagg." They had been neighbors for many years. Tocci lived at the point where Andrea skated, and Sterling and Popper before them; they skated home from this point with their coats open like sails. All the Taggs knew Tocci, but Tocci didn't know a Tagg by name, even after Sterling probably saw to the gash on the man's car.

Andrea kept watching her father. Sterling didn't do this kind of thing. He didn't go out of his way to provoke people. This might be the only time he'd ever done it.

"Rights to the high-water mark," Sterling said again.

Andrea worked, but she watched her father, too. She didn't think he picked Tocci's for the good clamming or to teach the guy about rights to clams. She thought it had more to do with Taggs' rights, or maybe rights to Taggs. Sterling was saying that Tocci didn't have any.

When the pail was filled, which they did almost in slow motion with each movement highlighted, they loaded up. Sterling started the motor, and they flew with the bow of the boat high in the water.

They flew to Heron Beach, where the clamming was choice. They pulled the boat up again and worked the flats on the crescent of beach, careful of the nesting colonies. They worked steadily. The sun came up. The sanderlings danced in the backwash.

"I don't know where she'll let us cook them," Sterling said.

"Never mind," Andrea said.

"I don't dare walk through the kitchen."

"I'll cook them."

"We ought to bring Pop down. He'd want to see the place."

Andrea nodded. She'd do that too.

"I held out a long time," Sterling said.

Andrea went to Esther's. It was Saturday. She had braided her hair. It reminded her of Swede to do that. A lot of Merry Maids were there, planning their itinerary. People were coming back to the island and business was good.

"How's it going?" It was Polly. She was at the counter. Andrea sat beside her. In front of them were Esther's variety-pack cereals that showed double in a mirror. Polly was so thin, Bess always used to say when she spent the night, she'd have to shake the sheets to find her. Whatever Polly had been doing, she hadn't been putting on any weight.

Polly was still dark and slight. Andrea was blond again, and long and jutting. Andrea looked at the two of them in the mirror.

"You were with Tom?" Andrea said.

"Yeah." Polly pressed her lips together over her braces and squeezed her eyes shut for a second.

Polly had a Hershey bar. She snapped off a square and slid the rest of the bar to Andrea. Andrea snapped off a square. She put it on her tongue and let it melt.

The regulars came in. Lester had an egg-and-bagel sandwich. Esther sang with the radio. Colonial people.

That same feeling came over Andrea that she had in the attic rafters: that she was for the most part alone. Andrea had her own fingers and eyes and tongue to taste. Polly had her own. Everybody at the counter had their own. People flashed around you with different tattoos like Queequeg had on his skin and they were a wonder. But nobody else had Andrea's fingers or her eyes or her tongue to taste.

They each had another square of chocolate. It tasted so good.

"Is Swede gone?" Polly asked.

"Yeah."

"It was looking serious," Polly said.

Andrea nodded.

Polly shook her head.

A horn blasted from the parking lot. The Merry Maids were forming up at their pickup. Polly slid off her stool.

"Did you ever want to get rich?" Polly said.

Andrea shrugged.

"We're short a girl."

She could do that, Andrea told herself. She could climb in that truck and earn a good day's pay.

"If you want to come, I'll tell Josephine," Polly said.

"All right," she said.

She went with Polly. Head Maid Josephine blasted the horn outside the cemetery gate. The Merry Maids' logo had a Mary Poppins sort of person with a dust mop reaching up to the clouds. She was painted on the truck's cab.

The truck was two-toned, purple and pink. It was strung with flags like a carnival and laden with girls and yellow-haired mops, a dog, silver pails, plastic buckets, bins of soap. If it began to sprinkle, Andrea imagined the pickup might explode with bubbles.

Andrea and Polly got in the truck. It stalled a couple of times and then glided down Main Street like a parade float. The dog barked, the girls sang, and the paper flags fluttered like birds' wings.

Bess left a letter on Andrea's dressing table. Andrea found it among her collection of arrowheads and World of Beauty potions and what her mother called junk. She was dirty and sweaty and pretty rich by the time she got home and found it. She took the letter down to the porch and read it, on the squealing glider swing.

Thursday morning

Andrea Tagg
Tagg Creek
Manhanset Island
Long Island
New York

Dear Andrea,
It's four in the morning. Are you up in my roof where I found you last night? No, it's been two nights. I just haven't slept. God, it seems like years. I keep trying to remember us there. I've spent the past about three hours looking for a pen because here I am in this lockup, ready to write with my own blood, I want to write you so bad. They got me quick and clean. The sergeant at the barracks says, "Oh, yeah, we been waiting for you, dude." So they call the MPs, who bring me here, and my Top comes dragging in and calls me names even you haven't heard of. He says I'm a felon, and even with a lot of hard talking to the company commander he doesn't know if he can save me. He says he hasn't met any-body stupid enough to hit a lieutenant since the draft. I think I make him nostalgic. I can't figure it, but he's getting a kick out of plotting the strategy. So he says, "You bastard, here's your *best*-case scenario." A bust. They take my one lousy stripe, cut my pay, and double my work for four months. Best case. All I

162

know for sure is that it's about dawn. They don't put a clock in here, either. I'm trying real hard to pretend it's a no-frills motel room. Top says they can't hold me here without a court order even after what I did. I get to go to the barracks and look at those four walls because I'm a lucky SOB, he says, and the Army's gone soft.

It must be almost dawn. About the time I was freezing my butt off outside—me and that blue chicken—and you were freezing yours off inside, and I climbed up to you. I found this pen in *A White Heron,* which I must have stuck in my inside pocket because it was there. Julie'll be madder than hell. You want to see if you can talk to her?

I think about you. I don't think we can live on my busted pay. I know you should be on the island, but that doesn't stop me thinking about you coming sometime. Or my getting back in four months. Best case. That's keeping me going tonight.

Love,<br>Swede

Andrea looked up and saw Eleanore on the porch steps watching her. She came in and sat on the glider, where they rocked and listened to the bell buoys ring.

FIC
FAR

Farish, Terry

SHELTER FOR A SEABIRD

FIC
FAR

33640000013023

Farish, Terry

SHELTER FOR A SEABIRD

ESEA-98